Peace
Treaty

Peace Treaty

Ruth Nulton Moore

Illustrated by Marvin Espe

HERALD PRESS
Scottdale, Pennsylvania
Kitchener, Ontario

Library of Congress Cataloging in Publication Data
Moore, Ruth Nulton.
   Peace treaty.

   SUMMARY: A young Moravian boy, captured by Indians near Fort
Duquesne, realizes he can use his faith to promote peace.
   [1. Moravians—Fiction. 2. Indians of North America—Fiction.
3. United States—History—French and Indian War, 1755-1763—
Fiction] I. Espe, Marvin. II. Title.
PZ7.M7878Pe   [Fic]   76-48922
ISBN 0-8361-1804-9
ISBN 0-8361-1805-7 pbk.

PEACE TREATY
Copyright © 1977 by Herald Press, Scottdale, Pa. 15683
   Published simultaneously in Canada by Herald Press,
   Kitchener, Ont. N2G 4M5.
Library of Congress Catalog Card Number: 76-48922
International Standard Book Numbers:
   0-8361-1804-9 (hardcover)
   0-8361-1805-7 (softcover)
Printed in the United States of America
Design: Alice B. Shetler

10 9 8 7 6 5 4 3 2

To my husband, Carl,
whose forefathers
were among the first settlers
in western Pennsylvania.

Contents

1
The Wagon Brigade

The wagon brigade wound slowly down the side of the mountain. Twelve-year-old Peter Andreas, the youngest member of the brigade, was bone-tired and foot-weary. All day he had walked alongside his uncle's team, leading the horses over the rough places on the narrow mountain road.

The top of the boy's auburn head blazed red in a shaft of sunlight that filtered down through the treetops. He paused for a moment to wipe the sweat from his forehead with the back of his hand. Would the long, hot day never end, he asked himself.

Above the horses' hoofbeats, the creaking of

9

leather, and the rumble of wagon wheels, his uncle's voice commanded, "Step lively, lad. You've been dawdling all day."

Peter stepped ahead grudgingly. It was just like Uncle Matt to say something like that. His uncle was never pleased, no matter how hard he tried.

But then, maybe Uncle Matt had a good reason for being impatient with him. Peter glanced down at the twisted fingers of his deformed hand. There wasn't much a boy with a crippled hand could do in his uncle's blacksmith shop.

He plunged his hand into the pocket of his homespun breeches and his twisted fingers touched the carving of the wooden lamb that his father had made for him before he and his mother had died. That was three years ago, just before Christmas.

After their deaths, Matthew Boyd had felt obligated to raise his sister's only child, although Peter could have stayed with the Moravian brethren in Bethlehem. So now on this August day in 1758 Peter was helping his uncle haul supplies west over the Pennsylvania mountains to General Forbes' supply base at Raystown. The wagon brigade had need of a good blacksmith with a sturdy wagon and Uncle Matt had volunteered his and Peter's services.

"Whoa, there! Whoa!" His uncle's shouts broke through the boy's thoughts. Uncle Matt pulled back on the traces and brought the team of six grays to a halt. Peter stretched himself up on his toes and looked ahead at the long line of covered wagons to see why they had come to a sudden stop. With their wheels and uprights a bright red and their white canvas tops blowing out like sails in the gentle breeze, the blue

10

Conestoga wagons made a pretty picture against the green slope of the mountain. Ahead of the lead wagon rode the escort of six buckskin-clad soldiers who guarded the brigade. On a big chestnut gelding sat Captain Newcombe, a long rifle nestled in his left arm.

"Sharp turn ahead!" the captain called back along the line of wagons.

The big Conestogas began to move on slowly. Going down the steep mountain was even worse than climbing it, Peter decided. On one side rocky cliffs rose steadily; on the other side the road looked down into a deep, tree-filled gully.

Uncle Matt climbed on the lazy board in front of the left back wheel where he could operate the brake.

"Whoa, there—easy Christopher!" he shouted to the lead horse when it was their turn to crawl around the bend.

Peter drew in his breath as he glimpsed, at the bottom of the gully, the wreck of a wagon, its flour casks scattered down the mountainside. With his good hand he clung tightly to the bridle strap to urge the team on slowly—ever so slowly. The wagon creaked and swayed as it inched its way around the turn. When it was finally around it, Peter let out a long breath of relief.

There were other steep turns ahead as the road twisted down off the mountain and it wasn't until the late afternoon sun had dipped behind the ridges to the west that they finally reached the wooded valley below.

Uncle Matt wiped his red face with his big blue handkerchief and mounted the wheel horse to ride a bit. Peter took his place on the lazy board to rest his weary feet. He closed his eyes but he couldn't shut out the image of wooded ranges heaving up all around him in blue and green swells, like windblown waves in a sea of wilderness. "No wonder they're called the Endless Mountains!" he told himself.

Uncle Matt took off his flat, broadbrimmed hat and fanned away a swarm of black flies that were buzzing around his head. "Appears like there's a clearing up ahead," he called back. "The sun's got an hour yet before setting but I reckon we'll be bedding down here for the night."

Peter opened his eyes and glimpsed a small stream alongside the road. He glanced beyond the stream to the dark trees of the forest. Even though they hadn't seen a sign of an Indian since they had left Fort Littleton, Captain Newcombe had warned the teamsters to be on their guard. All that summer there had been rumors of Indians loyal to the French spying on the advance of English troops and supply wagons crossing the mountains. Uncle Matt and the other drivers always kept their rifles loaded and ready.

Peter stared long and hard at the dark trees. Had he glimpsed a moving shadow through their dimness? Was it a deer or a wild turkey come to the stream to drink? The shadow slipped back into the forest and Peter sucked in his breath. It was no deer nor wild turkey nor any other creature. It was the shadow of a man wearing feathers!

"Uncle Matt!" he gasped. "I reckon I saw an Indian over there. Yonder by the run!"

Matthew Boyd swung around on the wheel horse.

He looked intently through the shadowy forest to where his nephew was pointing. Then he turned back again and shook his head.

"I don't see nary a thing but trees over yonder." His voice hardened. "You must have dust in your eyes, lad."

Peter blinked his eyes. The shadow had vanished. *Had* he just imagined that he had seen an Indian through the trees?

He was relieved when Captain Newcombe called a halt in the clearing and the wagon train made camp for the night. Uncle Matt slid down from the wheelhorse. The lead horse and the other grays drooped their heads in the August heat.

"Set the brake, Peter," Uncle Matt ordered.

Peter dropped the heavy block of wood, bound by a thick chain, underneath the back wheel. After making sure the brake held the big wheel securely, he jumped off the lazy board and hurried to the front of the wagon to help his uncle unhitch the team. Uncle Matt threw the traces over the backs of the horses and led them down to the stream to water.

"There's a locust thicket back yonder across the run," he called over his shoulder. "Get some locust cut for the horses by the time I have the cook fire ready."

Peter glanced anxiously across the run to the dark woods. "Uncle Matt, do you reckon there could be any Indians hereabouts?"

"Now boy, I wish you'd get over worryin' about Indians all the time." There was a hint of anger in his uncle's voice. "You've been pestering me about them ever since we started out. Now get going!"

Peter started on a run. He ran back along the

13

stream until he spied the locust thicket on the other side. Jumping from rock to rock he landed on the opposite bank.

"Howdy!" rang out a friendly call from the shadows of the thicket, and Peter recognized the familiar voice of the young wagoner from the North Carolina frontier.

"Howdy, Daniel Boone," he called back.

The young man grinned at him then went about his task of gathering locust.

Daniel Boone was used to mountain travel. He had gone west to the Ohio Valley with General Braddock's wagon brigade three years ago and he knew the ways of the French Indians better than any man in Captain Newcombe's brigade.

Peter glanced around him at the dark forest and said in almost a whisper, "Daniel, you have a sharp eye for Indians. Did you see any on the trail today?"

The young wagoner straightened up and looked at Peter. "Not today, I reckon. But I've seen a fair amount down in the Yadkin Valley where I come from and at the Forks of the Ohio where we fought the French." He gave the boy a long look. "Why are you so afraid of Indians, Peter?"

Peter glanced down at his dusty boots. He guessed by now the whole wagon brigade knew of his fear, his black, unreasoning terror of Indians. He took a deep breath. "I reckon it's because of my folks," he replied. "Three years ago they were Moravian missionaries to the Indians at Gnadenhuetten, the mission station back East along the Lehigh River. While they were at Gnadenhuetten, I was living in Bethlehem with the Moravian brethren and sisters. It was safer there for the children of the missionaries."

"Three years ago!" Daniel Boone interrupted. "I remember that fall and winter of '55. It was just after Braddock's defeat at the French fort, Duquesne, at the Forks of the Ohio. After that the whole Pennsylvania frontier was open to attack by the French and their Indian friends."

He leaned close to Peter and said in a low, confiding voice, "I don't mind telling you, Peter, that I was as scared of them then as you are now. When they and the French ambushed us at Fort Duquesne and came whooping and hollering from behind trees and bushes, I left my wagon and ran. I didn't stop running till I landed in Virginny."

Peter's eyes were wide. "You did?"

The young wagoner nodded solemnly. "Now get on with your story."

"Well," said Peter, "because the Moravian Indians at Gnadenhuetten refused to join the Delaware and Shawnee war parties, the mission was burned by a French Indian raiding party and my parents were massacred along with the Moravian Indians and the other missionaries."

Daniel Boone gave a low whistle. "Reckon I understand now why you fear them so."

Peter brought out the wooden lamb from his pocket. "My father carved this for me at Gnadenhuetten. One of the survivors of the raid found it and gave it to me that Christmas." He swallowed the lump that rose in his throat. "It—it's the only thing I have from my father."

Daniel Boone examined the carving closely. "I reckon I've never seen such a pretty thing as this," he said. "Your pa must have been a mighty fine wood-carver."

"He was," Peter said proudly. "I wish I could carve like him." It had been Peter's deepest desire to be a wood-carver like his father. But with a crippled hand— He sighed and put the carving back in his pocket.

Daniel Boone clapped the boy across the shoulder and gave him a little shove. "Now don't you fret none about Indians" he said. "Our new army under General John Forbes will soon be marching to the Forks of the Ohio again. This time we'll capture Fort Duquesne and clean them out. Just you wait and see!" He gathered up his locust branches and splashed back across the run.

Alone in the thicket, Peter noticed how still the forest had suddenly become. Except for one bird chirping off and on through the trees and the whinny of a horse somewhere along the run, not another sound could be heard. He gathered an armful of locust boughs as quickly as he could and started back toward camp. Halfway through the thicket he paused in mid-stride. The whinny of the horse sounded closer. He swung around. Glancing through the trees, his eyes caught a flash of gray along the run.

A horse must have strayed from camp. But then he glimpsed a moving shadow leading the horse. His blood froze in his veins. This time he was sure he wasn't imagining what he saw. The shadow was the shape of a man wearing feathers!

"An Indian!" he gasped. "An Indian running off with one of the horses!"

The Indian must have been following the wagon

16

brigade when they came down off the mountain, Peter reasoned.

A knot of fear grew tight in Peter's chest as he watched the Indian and the horse. He dropped his branches and leaped out of the locust thicket. He had to get back to camp and be quick about it or they might never see him nor the horse again.

He splashed across the run and raced through the tall trees, his heart thumping wildly as he ran. A few more yards and he would be within shouting distance of the camp.

He drew in a deep breath to yell out a warning when a hard hand came down over his mouth, choking him and muffling his frantic cry for help. Strong arms pressed around him like a vise and the next thing he knew, he was being dragged across the run and back into the forest.

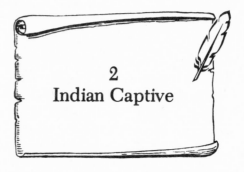

2
Indian Captive

Peter was so terrified that for a moment he couldn't move a muscle; he just dragged his limp legs after his captor. Then in panic he tugged and pulled at the arms that held him rigid, but the more he struggled, the more the arms, like bands of iron, tightened their hold. In desperation Peter bit into the flesh that covered his mouth. There was a grunt of pain and with a surprised cry his captor jerked his hand away. In that instant Peter leaped to his freedom.

He tore blindly through the trees with the angry pursuer close on his heels. He ran like the wind, on flying feet along the bank of the stream. He did not

18

see the tangle of grapevines hidden along the ground until it was too late and he tripped and went sprawling head over heels into a thicket. In an instant the Indian was upon him, flashing a tomahawk above the boy's head.

Peter froze with fear as he stared up at the fierce face. The Indian pointed back to the dark trees and said in a deep, steady voice, "Go quiet!"

A few yards away the Indian Peter had seen with the captured horse stood waiting for them. He was a thin, gaunt-looking old man. A necklace of bear's claws hung around his wrinkled neck. A cluster of eagle feathers, like those of a chief, dangled from his scalp lock. When he saw them coming, he urged the frightened horse on through the forest.

Peter and the brave followed. As he stumbled along, Peter felt as if he were walking in a nightmare. He could hardly believe it was all true, that what he had always feared was happening, that he was being captured by Indians!

He strained his ears for the sounds of Uncle Matt or Captain Newcombe coming to his rescue. But the forest was deadly silent. Not even a gunshot echoed from the camp.

They don't know I've been captured, Peter thought. How long would it take them to find out and come searching for him, he wondered.

The Indians were in a great hurry to get away. They followed the run for a mile or so until they came to a vague trace that threaded its way over a hemlock-covered hill. Once on the trail Peter was urged on relentlessly by the brave behind him. Farther and farther from the wagon brigade they

19

were taking him. And night was coming on!

Peter's legs, already tired from the hard day's walk, ached unmercifully and his feet felt like blocks of lead in his heavy, cowhide boots. When he stumbled over a tree root and fell face down in the middle of the trail, he knew he could go no farther. No matter what they did to him, he could not get up.

He closed his eyes tight and waited for the tomahawk to crack down on his head, ending his misery once and for all. But instead he felt himself being jerked to his feet and dragged over to the horse. The younger Indian pushed him up onto the big gray's back and walked alongside the horse while the old one led the way along the dim trace.

The first bright stars shone in the evening sky when they finally stopped along the edge of a deep ravine. Cupping his hands to his mouth, the old chief hooted three times like an owl. Peter shivered as he listened to the eerie call. He knew it must be a signal of some kind. Daniel Boone had told him that Indians often made "owl talk" when they were signaling to one another in the forest at night.

The dark ravine was silent as the call echoed away in the distance. Then, a few minutes later, another "owl" hooted three times in answer. The old Indian grunted with satisfaction and led the way down into the gully.

A faint flicker of light through the dark trees led them to a clearing where three other Indians and their frightened young captive were standing around a small campfire. By their appearances Peter guessed that they were a raiding party returning from the Pennsylvania frontier. One of the braves had a white

In a low voice he whispered, "I'm Peter Andreas. What's your name?" The girl stared at him with blank eyes.

woman's shawl tied around his shoulders with several pewter spoons stuck in it. On his belt thongs hung a scalp of long honey-colored hair. Another tall warrior had a man's broadbrimmed hat cocked on the top of his head and a scalp of short black hair hanging from his belt thongs.

When Peter glimpsed the two scalps, he felt his stomach turn over. Quickly he turned his eyes to the third Indian who was guarding an iron pot filled with the loot from a white settler's cabin. Standing in the shadows behind the fire was their captive, a frightened, pale-faced girl about the same age as Peter.

Peter stared at the white girl. Her homespun dress was torn and her bare legs were red with brier scratches. She stared back at him with wide, frightened eyes.

The Indians pushed the children roughly to one side and busily began unloading their packs. Peter moved closer to the girl. Never before had he longed for the company of a white girl as he did now. In a low voice he whispered, "I'm Peter Andreas. What's your name?"

The girl stared at him with blank eyes. In a voice that was dull and lifeless, she replied, "My name's Sarah Turner, but folks back home call me Sally. We were in our cabin in Cove Valley when the Indians came. The one over there led me away while the others killed Ma and Pa and raided the cabin."

Peter forced a glance over at the two scalps hanging on the Indians' belt thongs. The girl's eyes followed his. Then with a burst of tears, she buried her face in her hands, her thin shoulders trembling violently as she sobbed.

For a moment Peter forgot his own fears. The bloody redskins! How he hated them! He tried to comfort the girl by talking to her.

"My folks were killed, too, in an Indian raid at Gnadenhuetten," he said grimly. "They were Moravians."

"Moravians?" she asked, still sobbing. "What are Moravians?"

"They are the Unity of Brethren who came here from Germany and Central Europe for religious freedom," Peter explained. "They settled in a town back East called Bethlehem. They're mostly missionaries who preach to the Indians."

Sally Turner lifted her tear-stained face in wonder. "They preach to Indians? Why, folks in Cove Valley where I come from would as soon talk to wolves as to Indians!"

"Moravian Indians aren't like that. They are Christian Indians," Peter explained quickly. "They live in our missions and some of our missionaries live in their towns."

"Like we'll have to do most likely," Sally said, her voice full of despair.

Peter drew closer to her and whispered, "Don't fret. Captain Newcombe and his soldiers will come after us. Hush now. Here comes old Bear Claws."

Sally stopped sobbing when she saw the old chief shuffle over to where they were standing. From a deerskin bag he took a handful of parched corn and offered it to the children. Peter, who could have eaten a bear steak when the wagon brigade had stopped to make camp, was not hungry now. He shook his head, and so did Sally Turner. The old chief

23

laid the corn before them and turned away.

After their scanty meal, the Indians tethered the captured horse to a stout pine at the edge of the camp and spread out their animal robes close to the fire. Peter sank back against the rough bark of a tree and closed his eyes. He pretended to be asleep, but all the time he was listening for the sound of Captain New-combe's men. Surely they must have missed him by now and would come searching for him!

He kept listening until his ears ached but all he heard were the murmuring voices of the Indians by the fire. Then another sound came to his ears, the sound of soft moccasined footsteps approaching.

Peter lay very still and held his breath as the footsteps drew nearer. He opened one eye and glimpsed an Indian bent over Sally. It seemed as if he was slipping something around the girl's wrists. The next moment his own crippled hand was being jerked from his pocket.

He heard a gasp of surprise as the Indian who had captured him stared down at the twisted fingers. The old Indian came to his side and stared too. In horror the younger Indian reached for his tomahawk but the chief quickly knocked the weapon from his hand. He took the rawhide from the young brave and slipping the loop tightly around Peter's wrists, he tied the other end to his own and lay down beside the boy.

Peter was grateful to the old Indian for saving his life, but now a new fear filled his mind. Would the rest of the raiding party want to keep a white boy captive with a crippled hand? What use would he be to them?

Stories of the cruel things Indians did to the captives they did not want whirled through his head. Would they torture him then burn him at a stake, he wondered.

Peter drew in a long trembling breath and tried to push his fears from his mind. He closed his eyes again but as weary as he was, he could not sleep.

Sally Turner wasn't sleeping either. He could tell by her muffled sobs. He knew she was thinking of her pa and ma as he had often thought about his own parents.

Now as he remembered his home in Bethlehem, it was like a dream, as though it had never existed. And when he thought about his mother and father, they, too, seemed like a beautiful dream. They had told him that many whites mistreated Indians, took their land, and abused them in many ways. His parents had insisted that he should love his Indian brothers. But after they killed his father and mother, he wondered how anyone could ever love an Indian.

He moved about restlessly on the cold ground, the leather thongs biting into his wrists. The moon came up over the edge of the ravine and lighted the forest with its cold shining. A deer stamped in the brush nearby.

Thoughts of home and of his mother and father vanished in the darkness like the stray breeze through the trees as Peter, too, dropped off to a troubled sleep.

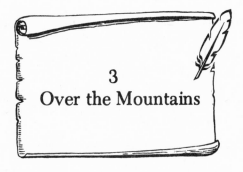

3
Over the Mountains

Dawn was beginning to break through the misty forest the next morning when Peter opened his eyes. For a moment he wondered what he was doing in this deep ravine, lying on the cold ground. Then he felt the sting of the leather thongs around his wrists and heard the whinny of the captured horse tethered on the edge of the clearing. He saw the Indians eating their breakfast of dried corn and jerky and saw Sally Turner sitting nearby, watching them. All that had happened the day before flashed like a bad dream through Peter's mind and a great heaviness swept over him.

Presently the old Indian came to his side. He unbound Peter's wrists and from a deerskin bag brought out a pair of moccasins and motioned for the boy to put them on. Sally came over and sat down beside him. Her eyes were no longer tear stained and Peter decided that she was all cried out. As much as she had sobbed during the night, he reckoned there wasn't another tear left inside her.

She was silent and Peter was aware that she was staring at his crippled hand. He quickly stuck it in his pocket.

"How did your hand get crippled?" she asked, "and why do you always keep it in your pocket?"

Peter looked away from her. "I was born with it that way," he said shortly. "It's no use to me, so why shouldn't I keep it in my pocket? Besides, the Indians will probably kill me for it since I won't be much use to them."

Sally shook her head soberly. "The Indians won't kill you, Peter, or else old Bear Claws wouldn't have given you a pair of moccasins to hike over the mountains in."

She stretched out her feet and Peter noticed that she was wearing Indian moccasins, too. "They're right pretty," she admitted, glancing down at the quillwork embroidered on the tops of them. "And they're soft, too. My feet were aching something terrible in my old shoes."

She glanced at the Indians around the fire and said in a hushed voice, "I thought you said your Captain Newcombe would come after us last night."

Peter's reply came in a voice filled with disappointment. "I guess he couldn't find our trail in the dark."

They fell silent as they watched the Indians break camp. After the men had loaded their heaviest packs on the horse, they gathered the rest of their gear and motioned for the children to get on their feet. As before, the old chief led the way with Peter and Sally following close behind him. The younger Indian and Sally's captors brought up the rear.

With the morning sun on their backs, they headed westward. The trail wound through forests of tall oaks and pines and across glades of high grass. The old chief set a fast pace.

"He aims to put as many miles behind him as possible," Peter grumbled to Sally.

"Where do you reckon they're taking us?"

"To one of their villages, most likely."

After that there was little talk between the two young captives. They had to save their breath to keep up with the Indians. But the moccasins did help. They were soft and light and made walking through the forest much easier.

All day they traveled, stopping only now and then for a drink by some fern-lined spring. Mechanically Peter put one foot in front of the other. Vaguely he was aware that ahead of them the beech trees, gilted by the later afternoon sun, stood out in the dimness of a wooded slope. They were climbing upward again, turning and twisting over rocks and fallen tree trunks. When they came to an outcropping of rocky ledges, the old chief stopped. He looked up at the sky and sniffed the air. Reluctantly he began taking the pack off his back.

Peter and Sally sank to the ground too exhausted to notice the rumble of thunder in the distance and the dark clouds closing in on the sun. They were so weary that both of them had to be dragged underneath the ledges when the big drops began to fall.

Some dried venison and parched corn were passed around. This time the famished children gobbled down the tasteless food. When Sally finished her rations, she huddled back against the cold rocks. "Why don't they light a fire?" she whispered.

"I guess they don't want to be seen from the valley below," Peter whispered back. "I reckon old Bear Claws wanted to get over this mountain before sundown but the storm stopped him."

"Then there must be a settlement down there," Sally reasoned, "but I don't know what settlement it could be this far off."

A sudden thought came to Peter. Could it be the fort at Raystown? Had they come that far?

Peter's thoughts raced. If he and Sally could get away tonight, they might be able to make their way down the mountain and find the settlement. If it was Raystown, they would be safe there until the wagon brigade arrived.

He was so excited with the idea that he wanted to tell Sally about it right away, but he would have to be patient and wait until the Indians bedded down for the night. He couldn't be sure how much English they understood.

Even with the storm it seemed to take forever for the last bit of daylight to fade from the mountainside. At last the Indians threw their robes on the ground and stretched out on them. Peter's ears rang in the silence that settled over the camp. Only the soft dripping of rain off the ledge broke the stillness.

"The rain is good," he thought. "It will hide our footprints."

Between lids that were almost closed, he turned to see if Sally was still awake. He couldn't tell in the dark. Slowly he began to crawl to her side to whisper his plans. Then he stopped short and his heart froze. Sally was bound to her captor like the night before, and it wasn't long before he felt the rawhide thong being slipped over his own wrists.

Miserable and cold he lay on the ground next to the old chief. He knew that one move of his hands to try to free himself and the old man would awaken. He let out a bitter sigh and stared out into the black night. There was no chance of escape now.

Sally Turner was mumbling her prayers to herself and Peter supposed that he should pray, too. But the disappointment at not being able to escape overwhelmed him and he didn't feel much like praying.

What good was prayer anyway? he thought bitterly. Often he had prayed that God would keep him safe from the Indians who had killed his parents. Why had God not answered his prayers?

Morning came too soon. Stiff and weary, their bodies still aching with exhaustion, the children were once more forced to follow the old Indian's fast pace up the side of the mountain. Not until they crossed over the crest and were coming down the other side, were they allowed to stop and rest.

They slumped to the ground and gazed over the unbroken wilderness of forests and mountains that stretched westward as far as they could see. Peter knew that when they climbed down the western slope of this ridge, Captain Newcombe would never be able to find them.

With despair he turned away from the scene and flung himself back against the trunk of a tree that had been partly uprooted by the storm. Sally seemed to sense how he felt.

"This old tree is kind of like us, Peter," she murmured, looking at the bare roots clinging desperately to the rocky soil. "We're uprooted, too, and I reckon we have to cling to life just like those old roots. Ma always said that the Lord never gives us more burdens than we can bear."

Peter turned away, feeling suddenly ashamed. After all she had just been through, Sally Turner had not lost her faith as he had almost lost his.

After they had climbed down the western slope of the ridge, the chief slackened his pace. They had left the last English settlement behind them. They were in Indian country now.

That day and for many days to follow they journeyed over the tall ranges of the Alleghenies and finally down the western slopes on scattered trails that only the Indians knew. Farther and farther from their homes they went, traveling steadily westward into a wilderness few white men had ever seen.

A day came when the trail ahead dipped steadily downward over a series of low rolling hills. They had left the mountains behind them, and now the highest ridges were but a blue haze on the far horizon.

One midafternoon the old chief paused on a rise of land and pointed to a long river valley that stretched out before them. Between dark wooded bluffs Peter and Sally saw two rivers joining together to form one long one that flowed northwest as far as the eye could see. And on the point of land where the rivers met sprawled the five arrowhead-shaped bastions of a fort.

"*De-un-da-ga*," the old Indian told them. He broke a branch from a nearby beech tree and drew the pattern of the rivers on the ground by their feet. He pointed to the right fork and spoke the word "Allegheny." He pointed to the left fork and called it "Monongahela." The great river flowing westward he called the "O-hi-o."

De-un-da-ga, the Forks of the Ohio!

The children studied the old Indian's crude drawing carefully then lifted their eyes to the grim-looking stockade carved out of the green of the wilderness valley.

"It's Fort Duquesne they're taking us to," breathed Sally.

"Fort Duquesne!" echoed Peter. It was a word spoken fearfully by every settler in the Back Country; for as long as the French fort commanded the Forks of the Ohio, no settlement in Pennsylvania was safe from Indian attack. Peter stared long and hard at the French fort. It looked gloomy and foreboding.

The old chief stamped out the design of the three rivers with his moccasins and motioned for the children to follow. Down the hill to the river flats they went, across a land that was marshy and desolate. On higher ground along the banks of the rivers were gardens and fields of corn. An Indian camp of thirty bark wigwams stood between the gardens. And beyond, surrounded by a log palisade, the five bastions of the fort rose up bold and stark against the gray river bluffs, an emblem of strength and terror.

On the edge of the Indian camp the old chief called a halt. The Indians untied the packs on the horse's back and drove the big gray into a log corral. They lingered outside the camp, talking together for a long while.

"I reckon now that they got us here, they're trying to decide what to do with us," Sally whispered in a trembling voice. She took Peter's hand in hers and held it tightly while they waited.

They were a sight to behold. Their clothes were torn and ragged and they were dirty and disheveled from the long trek over the mountains. But they were both so weary that they did not care anymore what they looked like. They shifted anxiously from one tired foot to another as they awaited their fate.

At last the old chief commanded them to follow him into the camp. Ahead ran the raiders, shouting their scalp hallos. The wild cries struck terror in the children's hearts.

Indian children gathered around the bewildered captives. They made faces at the two white children, laughing and poking their fingers at them, pulling at their hair and ragged clothes. In a large open space in the center of the camp the old chief separated Peter and Sally.

Beckoning Sally to come with him, he led her to a wigwam on the far side of the camp. Pulling back the heavy bearskin that served as a door flap, he ordered the white girl to enter. As she stepped inside, Peter couldn't see her anymore. But she told him later what took place.

The wigwam was built of a rough framework of poles overlaid with bark and animal skins. Tears came to her eyes as Sally glanced up at the bunches of herbs that hung from the roof poles to dry for winter's use. They were the same sweet-smelling herbs that had hung in her mother's cabin loft at home—sassafras, spearmint, and wild cherry bark. In the middle of the wigwam was a fire pit with a hole in the roof directly above it for smoke to go through. And behind the fire pit sat a fat, brown-eyed squaw stirring a kettle of stew.

When the squaw saw the ragged white girl, she arose and from a large basket woven of sweet grass she brought out a doeskin tunic and a pair of fringed leggings. She dressed Sally in the Indian clothes and combed her hair, braiding it in one long braid that hung down her back. When she was finished, she gave Sally a wooden ladle and pointed to the kettle of stew.

Sally dipped the ladle into the kettle and slowly sipped the hot stew. It was corn and meat and tasted wonderfully good. After she had eaten her fill, Sally sank down heavily on the bear robe by the fire. Tired, oh, so tired, she fell at once into a deep sleep.

She dreamed about a cozy cabin far away in Cove Valley. She dreamed about her mother singing her to sleep and her father smiling down at her from the wooden bench by the fire. It was the same dream Sally Turner would have over and over during the many lonely nights to come.

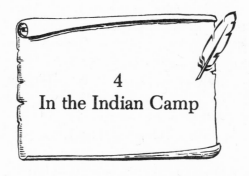

4
In the Indian Camp

Peter felt very much alone as he watched Sally Turner being led away by the old chief. With the leader gone, the younger Indian assumed command over the raiding party. He kept a close watch on Peter and now and then his eyes sought Peter's crippled hand hidden in his pocket.

"He won't forget that," Peter thought gloomily. "He's probably thinking up some trick to get rid of me, now that the old chief's not here."

At their leader's command the Indian women and children gathered sticks and switches then joined the men to form a double line across the open space.

Peter felt his throat tighten as he watched. So this was what his captor planned for him—to run the gauntlet!

Peter had heard of Indian captives having to run the gauntlet and being beaten to death. His heart pounded as he watched the double lines form, but as frightened as he was, he tried not to show it. Daniel Boone had once said that Indians admired courage more than anything else and that if a captive showed he was not afraid, it would go better for him.

Before he had time to think more about it, Peter felt himself being pushed into the double line of angry Indians. In an instant a wild cry went up as sticks and switches rained down on his head and shoulders.

Peter made a desperate attempt to pull back but the Indian leader kept pushing him through the line.

He floundered on, stumbling with the heavy blows, trying not to cry out with the sting of switches laid against his shoulders. He felt a trickle of blood run down his cheek from a cut on his head. As he plunged forward, a foot reached out to trip him. Sinking to his knees, he was pelted unmercifully. He thought this would be the end. No matter how fast he could run, he would never be able to make it through this howling line!

Then amid the wild shrieks and cries around him a voice called out in English. "Get up, white boy! Run or they will kill you!"

Peter could not see who had spoken the words but they told him that someone in this angry gathering was on his side. The words warmed him and brought back his courage. Struggling to his feet and shielding his head with his arms, he plunged on through the lines.

He stumbled again, but the voice kept urging him on. "Run, white boy! Run fast! Run to nearest wigwam!"

Shutting his eyes and gritting his teeth, Peter surged on, stumbling, getting up, stumbling again. Then he realized that no matter how much that friendly voice urged him on, he could never make it to the end of the line. There was only one thing to do. With the last of his strength, he swung around and flung himself at the nearest squaw. With a surprised grunt the woman lost her balance and Peter dashed past her through the opening in the line.

A cry of outrage arose as the Indians broke their lines and ran after him. Peter raced on toward the nearest wigwam. Just in time he reached it and fell groaning through the bearskin door flap. Gasping for breath, he dropped to the dirt floor exhausted. His vision blurred and his mind went spinning, then everything went black.

When he awoke, his head throbbed and he ached all over. He looked up and the face that bent over his came into focus. Seeing the long black hair, the low forehead, and narrow eyes, he screamed with horror and tried to pull away, but firm and gentle hands pushed him back on the pallet of furs.

"Lie still," a voice commanded. "Little Wolf will not harm you."

Something familiar in the voice caught Peter's attention. Then he remembered. It was the same friendly voice that had helped him run the gauntlet!

Peter stared up at an Indian boy not much older than himself. The youth was dressed in nothing but a breechcloth that hung across his lean loins and a pair of beaded moccasins on his feet. His dark skin, rubbed liberally with bear's grease, gleamed like copper in the light from the fire pit. A black wolf, the emblem of the Wolf Clan of the Delawares, was tattooed on the right side of his chest.

"You—you speak English," Peter struggled to say through swollen lips.

The Indian boy nodded proudly. "Little Wolf is the son of a chief. I have learned English from the Moravian missionaries who came to our village of Wyoming. For many moons they lived with us in Wyoming."

Wyoming! Peter had often heard Brother Joseph and the other Moravian brethren talk about the Indian town north of Bethlehem where a friendly clan of Delawares lived.

"I—I'm a Moravian," he struggled to explain.

The Delaware boy smiled. "Moravian brothers are good. They taught our Wolf Clan about the Great Spirit and His Son Jesus. Moravian brothers teach peace and that all men should love and respect one another. They made our Wolf Clan Christians."

Peter gave the Delaware boy a puzzled look. If Little Wolf was a Christian and a Moravian Indian as he said he was, what was he doing here in this hostile camp so far away from his village?

The Indian boy seemed to read the white boy's thoughts. He explained, "Chief Teedyuscung, leader of all the Delaware clans east of the Endless Mountains, has agreed to sit at a council fire at the Forks of the Delaware River and talk peace with the English. Our White Brother brings Teedyuscung's big hello to the Delawares, the Shawnees, and the Mingoes at

De-un-da-ga. My father and I came here with our White Brother to help him with his peace mission."

Peter closed his eyes and moved his head from side to side. Was the Indian boy making all this up? Was he just jabbering lies to impress the white boy captive? Everyone knew that the Delawares, the Shawnees, and the Mingoes, who lived along the Ohio, were Indians who liked the French and fought for them. They weren't at all friendly to the English like Teedyuscung's Delawares back East. What white man would dare to bring Chief Teedyuscung's peace talks to these tribes? Why, he'd be killed just as Peter's own father and mother had been at Gnadenhuetten!

Little Wolf made a poultice of balsam and laid it on Peter's head. "White boy did well running the gauntlet," he said with praise. "All boy and men captives must run it. It proves they are brave and worthy of being adopted into the Delaware tribe. The one who brought you here will adopt you."

Peter opened his eyes and groaned. "But I don't want to be adopted by him!"

The Indian boy looked at him gravely. "He lost a brother in the last war with the English. You are to take that dead brother's place. When you are well, you will live in his wigwam with his squaw."

Peter turned his head to the bark wall. He would never allow himself to be adopted by an Indian, he vowed, no matter how hard they tried to make him one of their own. The poultice of balsam began to ease his throbbing head and he drifted off to sleep again.

When he awoke the Indian boy was gone and an

old squaw was by his side. She ladled some broth from a kettle by the fire and put the ladle to his mouth. He sipped the broth slowly. It was rich and warm. He drank several ladlefuls then sank back on the fur pallet.

For several days Peter lay by the fire while the old squaw cared for him. On the fourth day when he managed to get to his feet, she left him a pair of deerskin leggings and a waistcloth.

Peter glanced down at his ragged clothes that the Moravian sisters has spun for him and woven and sewed. They were the last reminders of home—except for the Christmas lamb that his father had carved for him.

He plunged his hand into the pocket of his pants and found the wooden lamb hanging loosely in the torn threads. He curled his fingers tightly around it. Before he left Bethlehem, Brother Joseph had told him that the carving was a precious thing and that he should always keep it to remember his father by.

"Remember, Peter, the lamb is the symbol of the Moravian Church," Brother Joseph had said. "It symbolizes peace and brotherhood, the two virtues the Moravians love most."

Peter studied the carving closely. His father had been a fine wood-carver, it was perfect in every detail. He swallowed the lump that rose in his throat as he slipped out of his familiar homespun pants and shirt and tucked the carving inside his Indian waistcloth.

Dressed in his new clothes, Peter walked stiffly around the wigwam. He was thankful no bones were broken. He hobbled to the entrance and

40

pushed back the door flap. Glancing about the Indian camp, he wondered how Sally Turner was faring.

He walked outside to where a group of children were playing a game of fox and geese. He stared hard at them but there was no girl with honey-colored hair among them.

In the open space he saw the squaws tending cooking pots hung over open fires. A few women were stretching animal hides on big wooden frames to dry in the sun. A girl pounded corn in a hollowed-out log. But Sally was not with them either.

Peter made his way to the wigwam where the old chief had taken her the day they had arrived in the Indian camp. No smoke rose from the lodge. It seemed empty. Curiously he pulled back the door flap and peered inside. Nobody was there and the stones in the fire pit were cold.

What had happened to Sally Turner, he wondered. Where had they taken her?

He turned to leave the empty wigwam when a long shadow fell over him. He stopped short and looked up then shrank inwardly. There, with a scowl on his face, stood his captor.

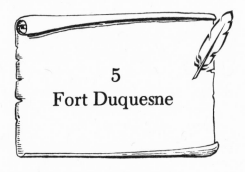

5
Fort Duquesne

The Indian who had captured him, took a step toward Peter and, grasping the boy by the arm, jerked him away from the wigwam. He motioned for Peter to follow him to the riverbank where a squaw was hoeing corn.

The Indian woman stopped her work and looked at them. His new foster father pointed to Peter and then to the long rows of corn. The squaw understood. She held out a stick with a sharp bone fastened to the end of it and motioned that Peter should start hoeing.

Peter took the crude hoe. He supposed this woman was the man's sister-in-law, the dead brother's squaw, and that he was to be her slave. Grudgingly he got to work in the hot cornfield.

Once, when he paused to rest, he looked back at the village, hoping to see Sally Turner. But there was no girl with honey-colored hair among all the black-haired children. He sighed and turned toward the riverbank that was lined with bark canoes. He watched a French bateau, a large canoe manned with three red-capped Canadians, drift by. He supposed that it was on its way to Canada to bring supplies to the fort. His eyes lingered on the bateau until the squaw ordered him back to work again. He was thankful when the sun set behind the high river bluff across the Monongahela and it became too dark to see the rows of corn.

The next day the Indian woman kept Peter as busy as before. After the rest of the corn was hoed, she sent him to the woods to gather sticks for kindling, and when the wood was gathered, she handed him two leather buckets and pointed to the river. Would she never run out of chores for him!

At the riverbank some boys were mending a canoe. Peter stopped to watch. They melted resin in a skillet and poured the hot pitch into a long crack in the bark of the bow. Peter was so interested in watching them that at first he did not hear a voice calling to him. It was not until one of the boys glanced up at him with a curious look that Peter's eyes gazed out over the river.

"White Boy!" the call came again.

Peter's heart leaped. It was Little Wolf!

He ran along the riverbank to meet the Delaware boy. Little Wolf pulled his canoe on the shore and held up a string of bullheads. "I'm going to the fort to trade these fine fish for some wampum," he said.

"Could I go with you?" begged Peter.

Little Wolf looked uncertain. Then glancing at the water buckets by Peter's side, he seemed to understand.

"If you go with me to the fort, the squaw will not find you!" His dark eyes twinkled. "Come, we'll use the back gate so she won't see you, White Boy."

"My name is Peter."

Little Wolf nodded. "That's a fine name. It's the same name the Moravian brothers gave my father when he was baptized. They call him Captain Peter because he's a chief."

"Where is your father now?"

"He's in the Indian camp telling the chiefs about our White Brother's coming. He is asking them to listen to what our White Brother has to say."

As they neared the fort, the boys stopped talking and walked in silence. Above them loomed the log walls of the palisade, high and foreboding. They passed the east gate with its drawbridge opening over a moat. When they came to the glacis, the slope leading up to the fort, they climbed it and dropped down into a dry ditch on the other side.

"When the fort is attacked, the French open the water gate to flood this ditch," Little Wolf explained. "Then when the drawbridge is up, the attackers cannot get into the fort."

They climbed out of the ditch and walked along the log stockade until they came to the back gate which was left open during the day for soldiers and Indians alike to come and go as they pleased.

Peter followed Little Wolf through the gate and

44

into the fort. It was like a little town inside. In the center was a parade ground surrounded by houses covered with bark. The large house by the drawbridge gate, Peter supposed, was the house of the commandant. Three of the bastions also contained buildings. The air was heavy from smoky coal fires and the walls were black with coal dirt, giving the fort a grim, cheerless appearance.

Peter followed Little Wolf to the storehouse and sat down on the door log while he waited for the Delaware boy to trade. He glanced up at the flag bastion where the white silk banner dotted with the *fleur-de-lis*, the three golden lilies of France, ruffled boldly against the blue August sky. In the other arrowhead-shaped bastions, bristling with cannon, blue-coated sentries stood idly watching the activities on the parade ground.

The fort was bustling with people. Indians, soldiers, and red-capped Canadians, some with heavy sacks slung over their shoulders, passed by Peter on their way in and out of the buildings. By the casemates and lean-to huts that lined the inner walls, women stood over large cooking kettles that hung over smoky coal fires. Another group of women and girls were chattering together by the well sweep in the middle of the parade ground.

Peter's eyes lingered on one of the girls who had long, honey-colored hair. Like the others she was dressed in a bright cloth skirt and bodice, with a white kerchief and a lace cap. There was something about her that made Peter stare. When she turned his way and he glimpsed her face, he drew in his breath. It was Sally Turner.

"Sally!" he called, leaping up from the door log and starting across the parade ground.

She ran to meet him, her eyes wide with surprise. "Oh, Peter, is it really you? At first I thought you were just another Indian boy."

Peter glanced down at his buckskin leggings. "I guess I do look like an Indian, dressed up in this garb." Then in a rush of words he asked, "Sally, what are you doing here?"

The girl glanced over her shoulder at the women still chattering by the well sweep. "The Indians who captured me brought me here to the fort," she explained. "That short, plump lady by the well is Madame Homet. She took pity on me and begged her husband, a French officer, to buy me from the Indians. The Homets have no children of their own so I reckon they have sort of adopted me. Madame Homet is real kind to me, Peter. She gave me this pretty dress to wear and is teaching me how to speak French, and every night we eat at Captain de Ligneris' table in the headquarters room. Captain de Ligneris is commandant of Fort Duquesne."

She paused to catch her breath and looked at Peter, her eyes full of concern.

"What about you? How did you get that lump on your head and all those bruises?"

Peter told her about the gauntlet, sparing her of the worst details. He told about the friendly Delaware boy, Little Wolf, and about his captor wanting to adopt him to take the place of his brother who was killed by the English.

"I've heard tell some Indians do that," Sally said. "When one of them gets killed in battle, they set out to capture a white person to take the dead one's place."

"I'd rather try to escape than be adopted by Indians," Peter grumbled.

Sally Turner shook her head sadly. "We'd never be able to find our way back over the mountains alone, Peter. We'd go hungry or else be devoured by wolves. Madame Homet says the wolves are fierce around here, and howl something terrible across the Monongahela at night."

Peter scuffed the ground with the toe of his moccasin. He knew in his heart what Sally Turner said was true. Finding their way back across the Endless Mountains alone would be impossible. The sound of a voice calling from across the parade ground broke through his thoughts.

"Sal-lee!"

The girl swung around. "I have to go now, Peter. Come to the fort again—promise?"

"I'll try," Peter said. He watched her start back to the well sweep. She turned once and waved. Then the short, plump woman put her arm around her and led her toward the officers' quarters in the north wall.

Peter walked slowly back to the storehouse. He was glad he had found Sally Turner at last and that she was safe here in the fort. He began to make plans how he could return the next day to see her again.

But the next morning the squaw had other plans for Peter. The sun had scarcely arisen when she ordered him to follow her to the river. She pointed to one of the canoes beached along the shore and when he got in, she pushed it off the bank and paddled across the water.

The current was swift and she had to paddle briskly so that they would not float out past the Point and onto the Ohio. It soon became apparent to Peter that they were headed for the long wooded island in the middle of the Allegheny.

When they reached the sandy tip of the island, the squaw paddled around it to the other side and soon the fort was out of sight. She beached the canoe and nudged Peter in the back with the end of her paddle to get out. She gave him a long pointed stick and a leather sack and motioned for him to follow her. In the shoals along the shore she showed him how to hunt for mussels and clams.

Peter waded through the shallow water, watching for tiny holes and air bubbles in the sand.

This is much easier than hoeing corn or gathering firewood or toting buckets of water, he thought. In fact he rather enjoyed splashing through the cool, shallow water.

When his sack was half full of shellfish and he could find no more where he was digging, he decided to search on the other side of the island. The squaw was too busy filling her own sack to watch him closely. She did not see him start up the beach and slip through the trees.

The island was well wooded and after walking a little way, he stopped to look around. It was peaceful here among the big trees, away from the noisy Indian camp. Only the hoarse cry of a wild goose winging over the treetops and the chatter of a busy squirrel on a limb above him broke the silence. He wished Sally Turner could be here to share this peace with him.

Then suddenly, up ahead, a twig cracked sharply.

48

Was someone walking softly among the trees? Peter stood very still and listened. The footsteps seemed to come from the grove of tall chestnut trees up ahead.

He crept on through the trees until he came to a clearing. He crouched behind some bushes and peered between the branches. In the middle of the clearing was the buckskin-clad figure of a man kneeling on the ground.

Peter's pulses quickened as he studied the stranger. He was dressed in moccasins, leggings, and an Indian hunting shirt. His hands were clasped together and he seemed to be talking.

But who was he talking to? Peter saw no one else in the clearing. He edged nearer to hear what the man was saying.

"Thank you, Lord, for this new day and for bringing me safely to this island," spoke the voice.

"Why, he's praying!" Peter gasped with surprise. Then he drew in his breath. The man was a white man—an Englishman!

When he finished his prayer, the man raised his head and put on his wide-brimmed hat. The look on his face was that of peaceful contentment, as if he were sitting before his own cabin door instead of in the middle of an uninhabited island.

Peter was so intent in watching the white man that he did not notice the sound of another footstep moving stealthily among the tall trees behind him.

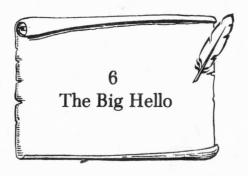

6
The Big Hello

Peter was about to rush into the clearing, present himself to the white man, and ask to be rescued from his Indian captors when a hand from behind grasped him by the shoulders and drew him back from the clearing.

Torn between fright and anger, Peter swung around to see who was holding him. "What are *you* doing here?" he cried out with surprise when he saw Little Wolf.

"I was about to ask you the same thing," the Delaware boy replied.

"I came with the squaw to gather shellfish," Peter

answered. "I didn't see you come to the island."

The Delaware boy's eyes danced mischievously. In a voice as low as a whisper he said, "You did not see me because I came ahead of the others and beached my canoe on the opposite shore."

"Ahead of the others?"

Little Wolf released his grip on Peter's shoulders and put a finger across his lips. He pointed back through the trees to the solemn procession of painted Indians and Frenchmen marching into the clearing. "If your new father is among them, you would not want to be seen here with the White Brother."

"The White Brother?" Peter stared at the man in the clearing. So this was the White Brother who was going to talk peace with the Ohio Indians. Peter studied the man closely. He didn't look much like the Moravian brethren. He was tall and lean with the appearance of a backwoodsman who might have lived with the Indians for a long time. His face was rough-featured as if hewn out of hard wood, but with all its rugged appearance, it wore the look of gentleness and understanding.

One Indian, a big, unpainted fellow, took his place next to the white man. His companion, a squat, shifty-eyed brave, joined him. Two older Indians stood on the other side of the man.

"Is he a captive?" whispered Peter. "What's his real name?"

"His name is Christian Frederick Post. He's a Moravian missionary and not a captive. But he's in great danger coming here. That's why he camped on this island and not in the village by the fort."

Christian Frederick Post didn't look as if he were in

51

danger. He stood as calm and as dignified as the two older Indians by his side. His piercing blue eyes flashed with interest at the Frenchmen and Indians who were gathered in the clearing.

"Today our White Brother brings Chief Teedyuscung's big hello to our brothers at Fort Duquesne," Little Wolf explained as the boys crept closer to the clearing.

Peter continued to stare at the white man. Like all Moravian missionaries he carried no gun. The only thing in his hands was a leather-bound Bible. Uncle Matt had said it was dangerous enough to go into Indian country with a gun, but *without* one—

"They'll kill him for sure," Peter muttered. "They look mean enough to do it."

Little Wolf shook his head. "He'll be safe as long as King Beaver is here to protect him. All tribes respect the king of the Ohio Delawares. He's ready to speak now."

The oldest of the four Indians who stood by Christian Post's side stepped forward. He was stooped and looked very ancient. Muddy wolfskins draped from his shoulders and hung to the ground. A great chain of white bone beads hung around his wrinkled neck and several eagle feathers were tied to his topknot. On his forehead he wore the turtle tattoo of the Unalachtgo Clan of the Delawares.

"What's he saying?" whispered Peter.

"He's presenting our White Brother to the chiefs who came over from the fort," Little Wolf answered quietly. "He says our White Brother has great news."

The gathering of chiefs listened to Beaver's words with respect, but when he finished speaking, they didn't stretch their hands, palms upward, to signify that they were glad to see the missionary. One brooding old Indian spoke out angrily, stamping his foot on the ground as he spoke.

"I do not know this Englishman. It may be that you know him. But I, the Shawnee, and our father, the French, do not know him. I stand here as a man on his own ground, I do not like it that an Englishman comes to our ground."

The French captain stepped forward. "What's he saying?" Peter asked in a low voice.

"He wants our White Brother to come to the fort," Little Wolf replied. "He says it is a custom among the white people that when a messenger comes to Fort Duquesne they blindfold him and lead him into the fort, to a prison cell or a private room."

As the Frenchmen started toward the Moravian missionary, Peter almost closed his eyes. He didn't want to see this brave man captured and taken to Fort Duquesne.

But old Beaver stepped in front of the French officers. He spoke out in an angry voice.

"It may be a custom among our father, the French, but the Delawares have no such custom. I, Beaver, king of the Delawares, brought the White Brother here for all to see and to hear what he has to say."

Turning to the old Shawnee, he said, "You have lived too many moons at the French fort. You don't think like an Indian but like a Frenchman."

Like the sound of a rising storm, a murmuring ran through the gathering of chiefs. Then one of them spoke up, "Let the White Brother speak. We will hear what he has to say."

Peter marveled at the missionary's sublime courage. His face was calm and there was even a gentle smile on his lips as he stepped forward to speak. The scowling Frenchmen drew back as the missionary addressed the gathering.

"Brothers of the Ohio, you know that the bad spirit has brought something between us that has kept us at a distance from one another. I now, by this wampum belt, take everything out of the way that the bad spirit had brought between us, and all the jealousy and fearfulness we had of one another. Let us look up to God and beg for His help, that He may put into our hearts what pleases Him and join us close in that brotherly love and friendship which our grandfathers had." A string of beads was placed at the feet of the Indians.

Then Christian Post read Teedyuscung's big hello: "Greetings, brothers. It is agreed that a white wampum belt of peace should be sent to you and that your leaders come to our council fire at the Forks of the Delaware where your brothers, the Delawares, and your cousins, the Six Nations, will meet with the English to talk of peace. I assure all, my brothers of the Ohio, that nothing would please me and all the people of Pennsylvania better than to see our nations at peace again. We pray to the Great Spirit that the hatchet be buried on both sides and that belts of peace be exchanged that we may live in brotherly love and friendship."

Christian Post placed Teedyuscung's white wampum belt with the string of beads before the Indians.

The French captain took a step forward again and glared angrily at the peace belts, but Christian Post

54

continued to speak to the Indians.

"Listen, brothers, the English king has sent a great number of warriors who are now on the march to the Ohio to avenge the blood that the French have shed. By this belt I take you by the hand and lead you at a distance from the French for your own safety that your legs may not be stained with blood. We look upon you as our countrymen who have sprung out of the same ground as we. We do not call you to war as the French do. We love you. We wish you may live without fear or danger with your women and children. Let the white men fight their own battles. Let all the Delawares and Shawnees and Mingoes join together with their eastern brothers in peace." Another large wampum belt was laid at the feet of the Indians.

"Brothers, one more thing I must ask. You know how sad it is if one loves a little child or a member of a family and somebody takes that loved one away. He will think about that one day and night. Since our loved ones are in captivity in Indian towns, we beg of you to let them return to the love of their families. Bring them to me and I shall stretch out my arms to received them kindly." A last string of wampum was placed by the others.

The Delawares took up the belts and laid them at the feet of the Mingoes. Their leader arose and told the Delawares, "What we hear our white brother say pleases us. Before the change of the moon we will meet with Teedyuscung and the Six Nations at the council fire at the Forks of the Delaware and hear what our brothers have to say."

In turn the Mingo leader handed the peace belts to

the Shawnees. "You brought the hatchet to us from the French and asked us to strike down our English brothers," he told the Shawnee leader. "You may consider why you did this."

The French captain watched the Shawnee leader closely. When the chief accepted the belts, he turned away angrily. With his soldiers he stalked back through the trees to his canoe beached on the shore.

The squat, shifty-eyed brave left Christian Post's side and joined the Frenchmen. "That's Shamokin Daniel, one of our White Brother's guides," whispered Little Wolf. "My father doesn't trust Daniel as much as our White Brother does."

The Indian chiefs followed but before they left, their spokesman told King Beaver that they would be back the next day with more Indians from the camp to hear what the White Brother had to say.

"Come. We must leave, too," Little Wolf whispered. "Boys are not supposed to listen at council meetings."

But Peter had no intention of leaving without speaking to the Moravian missionary and asking for his help. He started out boldly for the clearing.

"Wait!" hissed Little Wolf, but the warning came too late. The big unpainted brave by Christian Post's side leaped through the chestnut trees and, grabbing both boys by the arms, marched them into the clearing.

Christian Post looked up with surprise when he saw the two boys. Recognizing Little Wolf, he turned to the Indian who stood with King Beaver and said, "Captain Peter, here is your son."

Little Wolf's father looked every inch a chief, Peter

thought. His black eyes were piercing and proud. He wore a hunting shirt richly embroidered with black and white beads. On his neck rested a necklace of bear claws. He frowned down at his son and spoke sternly, but even this he did with dignity.

"You know, my son, that boys are now allowed at council meetings."

Little Wolf looked at his father but said nothing.

"Perhaps Little Wolf can be useful to us, now that he is here," Christian Post put in cheerfully, his flashing blue eyes smiling. "He can gather firewood and start a fire for our supper."

He waited for the chief to give his consent and when Captain Peter nodded, the Indian boy smiled gratefully at the missionary.

"Who else have you found on this island, Prisquetomen?" Christian Post asked his guide.

Prisquetomen pushed Peter forward. Christian Post looked closely at him then said with surprise, "Why, you're a white boy! Can you tell us who you are, lad?"

Now that Peter had a chance to speak, he felt tongue-tied. With Prisquetomen's enormous hand still gripping his arm, he thought he'd never be able to tell his name. But the gentle eyes of the missionary urged him on.

"Peter Andreas, sir, of General Forbes' wagon brigade," he blurted out. "I was captured by French Indians back near Raystown, on the other side of the Alleghenies." Then in a rush of words he told Christian Post what had happened to him in the Indian camp across the river. He told about Sally Turner, who was a prisoner in Fort Duquesne.

"Could you help us escape, sir?" he pleaded. "Could you take us away with you?"

Christian Post's face lost its smile, but he held out his hand to the boy. "So many prisoners in the Indian towns I visited have begged me to help them, but their masters would not let them go. If your masters do not find you, you are welcome to stay in my camp, Peter. But my life among my Indian brothers is no safer than yours and you'll have to take the same risks I do."

Peter's heart warmed to the missionary's words. Christian Post continued. "I must warn you, Peter, that it might be safer for you to remain at Fort Duquesne until General Forbes and his army come to claim the fort. Then all prisoners will be freed. The general hopes to arrive here before winter sets in and snows close the trails. By God's grace, I hope before then to have won over the confidence of the French Indians so that I can assure Teedyuscung and the Six Nations that their western brothers will listen to the peace proposals of the English. The French depend greatly upon their Indian allies. If a peace treaty is signed with all the Indian nations, it will help end this terrible war."

Peter's head was whirling at what Christian Post was telling him. Peace with the French Indians! Was it possible? Could one man perform such a miracle?

The missionary seemed to be reading the boy's thoughts. "I've lived many years with our Indian brothers, Peter. I'm one of them, for I love and trust them and they love and trust me. Preaching God's Word has made it so."

Christian Post held up his leather-bound Bible.

"You see, lad, this is my weapon—the only one I will carry into the wilderness. It is God's Word and it *does* work miracles. It's much stronger than the sword or the rifle."

Peter stared at the Bible. He had been taught by the Moravian brethren and sisters that God's Word was strong and could work miracles. He turned his eyes away from the missionary, ashamed of his own lack of faith.

"The choice is yours, Peter, whether you wish to stay with me or return to the Indian camp," Christian Post said kindly. "Think it over while you help Little Wolf gather some firewood. There's driftwood along the shore. It's easy to gather and makes a good fire."

When the boys came out of the woods, Peter noticed that the squaw was on the sandbar, putting her sack of shellfish into the canoe. He paused a moment then ducked down quickly and began to gather pieces of driftwood, hoping that she wouldn't see him. But out of the corner of his eye he glimpsed her coming toward him.

Grabbing his load of firewood, Peter ran back through the trees. When he reached the clearing, he tried not to notice that the squaw had followed. He hurried about piling the driftwood on the ground so that a fire could be built under it. The squaw came up to him and pulled at his arm.

Peter looked up helplessly. Nearby stood Christian Post. At that moment the tall missionary looked like a fortress to Peter. He jerked his arm free from the squaw's grasp and ran to stand by his side.

The squaw pointed toward the river and scolded Peter with sharp Indian words. Christian Post took a step forward and spoke to her sternly. Casting a threatening look over her shoulder at Peter, she slunk back through the trees.

His eyes shining, Peter looked up at Christian Frederick Post. At that moment he forgot the dangers that might lie ahead if he joined this daring missionary. He knew only that here was a man he'd be glad to follow. He had made his choice. Come what may, he would cast his lot with the tall missionary.

7

The Delaware Traitor

That night there were six camping on the island in the Allegheny—Christian Post; his faithful guides, Prisquetomen and Captain Peter; King Beaver; and Little Wolf and Peter. Shamokin Daniel, the other guide, had not returned from the fort.

Peter sat by the campfire next to Little Wolf and listened to the strange talk of the Indians. He was getting used to King Beaver's wild, shaggy appearance, animal-like in his wolfskins, and Prisquetomen's stern countenance, as if his face was hewn out of brownstone. They were now his companions and gradually his fear and distrust of them disappeared.

Prisquetomen was talking, his frowning face looking more stonelike than ever as the flames of the fire played upon it.

"Prisquetomen doesn't like it that Shamokin Daniel went across with the Frenchmen," Little Wolf leaned over and whispered to Peter. "Like my father, he doesn't trust Daniel."

Christian Post answered his guide in the Delaware dialect.

"Our White Brother says that Shamokin Daniel told him he was going to the fort to get some bread for us," Little Wolf continued, "but I don't think my father and Prisquetomen believe that's the real reason he went with the Frenchmen."

The talk continued on into the night. Then Christian Post read a passage from his Bible and, raising his hands, gave the benediction. The dark trees made deep shadows around him but the flames from the fire brightened the missionary's face. The Indians bowed their heads and murmured "Amen" in unison at the close of the benediction. And although Peter had not understood a word, a feeling of wonder came over him. Never before had a benediction seemed so real or meant so much to him.

When the fire burned down to red coals, the boys rolled up in robes of rabbit skins and lay close to the burning embers. Little Wolf dropped off to sleep at once, but Peter kept blinking at the fire, his mind going over all the strange things that had happened to him that day. Little would he have guessed, at the beginning of the day, that this night he would be sleeping on an island in the middle of the Allegheny with a Moravian missionary and an Indian king. He let out a long sigh. For the first time since he had been captured, he felt free.

A footstep sounded near his robe and a dark shape bent over him. Instinctively he sat up, but a hand reached out to quiet him.

"It is only I, Christian Post, Peter," a low voice said. "I saw that you weren't asleep. So many nights I, too, have lain awake by the fire, thinking. Tonight I was thinking that perhaps it is God's will that we have come together in this strange place."

"God's will?" Peter questioned.

"Yes, Peter. God has a plan for us all."

Peter raised himself up on his elbow and thought for a moment. Was everything part of God's plan? He thought about his parents and the massacre at Gnadenhuetten. Was that part of God's plan, too? He questioned the missionary about it.

"I remember that terrible time three years ago," Christian Post answered. "Yes, even death is in God's plan, Peter. Wasn't that so with our Savior? Sometimes God's will seems strange—and even cruel—but it is a part of His greater plan. The sufferings of the present are not worth comparing with the glory of heaven that is revealed to us in the Scriptures."

"Then you're not afraid of death, sir?" Peter ventured to ask.

"No lad. My life is in God's hands. He will do with it as He wills. It is not we who are important; it is why we were placed on this earth that matters. We all have a destiny and we must accept what it is. You should be proud of your brave parents, Peter, for they died in God's name."

The missionary touched Peter's hand with his own then drew away into the darkness.

Peter lay very still for a long while thinking over what Christian Post had told him.

A plan—a destiny. What could God's plan be for him here in the wilderness, he wondered.

The echo of the morning gun at the fort, rolling up the river canyons, awakened Peter the next day. The others were already up and Prisquetomen had some fresh perch broiling over the fire. The tantalizing smell of the fish made Peter fold his robe in a hurry and take his place with the others by the fire.

That day a great many more Indians, almost three hundred in all, came across the river to hear what the white brother had to say. Little Wolf was in a happy mood that so many had come from the Indian camp to listen to Teedyuscung's big hello.

"What our White Brother told the chiefs yesterday must have pleased them," he told Peter on their way to the shore to gather more driftwood. "If the treaty at the Forks of the Delaware is signed, all the tribes east and west will live in peace with the white man."

Peter was happy at the turn of events, too. There was only one thing that bothered him. It was Sally Turner, who was still a prisoner of the French at Fort Duquesne. Peter knew he could not leave with Christian Post unless he first helped Sally escape.

Little Wolf was puzzled at the white boy's brooding. "What is troubling my brother?" he asked.

Peter spoke his thoughts. "I must go to the fort and tell Sally Turner that I am no longer a captive. I must help her escape, too."

"Pretend to be looking for shellfish," the Indian boy said.
"If anyone is watching, they'll think we're just fishing."

Little Wolf frowned. "It will be too dangerous for you to leave the island now. They might see you and capture you again."

But Peter had made up his mind. "I must go," he declared.

The Indian boy shook his head, but Peter paid no attention to his protests. He kept glancing across the river at the fort, trying to think of a way to rescue Sally.

"I will paddle a canoe across the river after dark," he said. "Then nobody will see me when I leave the island."

"The gates to the fort are closed and barred for the night," Little Wolf told him. "You'll have to go over before sundown if you want to get into the fort."

A long silence hung between the two boys. How could he get across the river in daylight without the risk of being seen from the Indian camp, Peter wondered. But, no matter what happened to him, he could not leave Sally behind. He must at least try to help her get free. He turned toward the canoes.

"Wait," the Indian boy said. "I think I know a way." He beckoned for Peter to follow him around the sandy tip of the island to where his own canoe was beached. He motioned for Peter to get in. Pushing the canoe into the water, he jumped in himself and started to paddle close to the shoreline.

"Pretend to be looking for shellfish," he told Peter. "If anyone is watching us from across the river, they'll think we're just two boys fishing."

Peter kept looking down at the shallow water, grateful that Little Wolf was willing to help him. When they came to the northern end of the island,

Little Wolf did not paddle directly across the river but let the canoe drift downstream to the point of land in the Forks. He paddled the canoe around the Point and beached it on a narrow sandspit on the Monongahela side.

"Keep close to the stockade walls," he warned as they climbed the steep bank that rose up from the Point.

They crept ahead until at last they came to the rear gate. They slipped through it and quickly mingled with the crowd on the parade ground. At the well sweep a soldier glanced idly at the two boys then turned away. They strolled past the casemates where women were busy preparing food over the cooking fires. They did not see Sally Turner with them, nor did they see her by the well nor anywhere else in the fort.

"She must be inside one of those houses," Peter said, pointing to the officers' quarters in the north wall.

"We can't go in there for her," Little Wolf warned.

"Maybe if we stay by the well sweep, she'll see us and come out," Peter suggested hopefully. "That's where I met her yesterday."

They were starting back across the parade ground when Little Wolf stopped short and nudged Peter. "Look!" he exclaimed, pointing to an Indian wearing a blue officer's coat and black hat. "Shamokin Daniel!"

Peter stared at the squat, shifty-eyed Indian. It was almost comic the way he looked with the long officer's coat hanging halfway down his bare, bowed legs and the three-cornered hat tilted over his scalp lock. He was strutting in front of some Indians by the east gate. In a loud voice he boasted, "See what the French father has given me. I was in Philadelphia and never received a farthing from the English."

Little Wolf glared at the Delaware guide with disgust and turned away.

"He's going into the commandant's house," Peter whispered.

Little Wolf swung around and stared at the guide again. "Let's see what he's up to," he said, "but wait until the guard isn't looking."

When the sentry turned his head, Little Wolf motioned Peter to follow. The boys slipped around the corner of the building. The window in the back wall was open to the cool afternoon breezes and they crawled quietly up to it. Standing on tiptoes, they peered into a room filled with officers. Pacing back and forth in front of a rough pine desk was the commandant himself. His black boots shone and his gorget glittered, as did the shiny buttons on his white coat edged with gold lace. Peter had never seen an officer dressed so elegantly. Captain de Ligneris stopped pacing when the door at the far end of the room opened and Shamokin Daniel entered.

After seeing all that they could, the boys crouched below the open window so that Little Wolf could hear what the commandant was saying to the Delaware guide.

"Have you found out where the missionary is going from here?" Captain de Ligneris demanded.

"Our White Brother goes up the Ohio to Kuskuski, the towns of the Delaware king," Shamokin Daniel replied. "He will give the Delawares of Kuskuski

Teedyuscung's big hello and more peace belts from the English."

"We must stop him, *Mon capitaine!*" an officer's voice broke in. "If the Delawares accept Teedyuscung's big hello, the tribes that are here at Fort Duquesne might desert us like the Mingoes."

"The Delawares and Shawnees will never desert!" Captain de Ligneris replied. "They know we are the strong ones. They have not forgotten how the English fled like frightened children before their tomahawks when Braddock tried to capture Duquesne three years ago."

"*Oui, mon capitaine,*" the officer argued, "but our Indian scouts tell us that this White Brother has strange powers over the Delawares."

Shamokin Daniel spoke up, crafty and demanding. "I am the White Brother's scout. He trusts me. Maybe I can help my father, the French." He paused and there was a heavy silence in the headquarters room. The next sound the boys heard was that of coins jingling on the desk top.

"Will that satisfy you?" the commandant's voice snapped.

"The French father is generous," was the Delaware traitor's raspy reply.

"Then how do you intend to help us?" demanded the commandant.

Shamokin Daniel answered, "I told our White Brother that I have come to the fort to get bread. When the sun rises again, I shall return to the island with the bread but I shall be accompanied by some, trusted warriors from the Indian camp. The White Brother and his guides will gladly let us into their

69

camp. Once there we shall fall upon them and bring the White Brother to the fort. I promise that tomorrow he will be your prisoner!"

Little Wolf did not wait to hear more. He sprang to his feet and motioned for Peter to follow.

"Hurry!" he hissed and there was high excitement in his whisper.

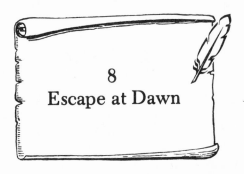

8
Escape at Dawn

In their haste to get away from the commandant's house, Peter and Little Wolf forgot about the soldier guarding the front. Hurrying around the corner of the building, they almost tripped over his feet.

The sentry gave a surprised shout and started after them. With Peter following hard on his heels, Little Wolf made a dash for the drawbridge gate.

The boys raced across the drawbridge and slipped down the bank into the dry moat. Together they huddled underneath the drawbridge and listened to the guard's heavy boots pounding across the loose boards above them. To the breathlessly waiting boys, it seemed like hours until the footsteps retreated back across the bridge. They listened until they were sure the guard was gone, then they made their way out from under the bridge and crept along the ditch until they reached the rear gate. With pounding hearts they scrambled out of the ditch and slid down the bank that led to the sandspit at the Point.

"Woh! That was a close one!" breathed Little Wolf when they came to where they had beached the canoe. "Hurry, let's leave this place before they send an army after us!"

Regretfully Peter looked back at the fort. He knew that this was no time to go back and look for Sally. As Little Wolf paddled rapidly across the river, he told Peter what he had heard from the commandant's open window. "We must warn our White Brother," the Delaware boy exclaimed.

When they reached the island, they hid in the chestnut grove and waited until Christian Post finished talking with the Indians who had come over from the fort. When at last the missionary was alone with his guides, the boys slipped into the clearing.

Christian Post listened gravely as Little Wolf told about Shamokin Daniel's plot to capture him. He shook his head sadly. "I mistrusted Shamokin Daniel even before we started across the mountains, but I thought when we arrived at Fort Duquesne, he would prove more faithful."

"He is a snake that speaks with a forked tongue," Prisquetomen said. "He has betrayed you, White Brother. We must leave this island at once."

Christian Post turned to Peter. "While you and Little Wolf were at the fort, several braves from the

Delaware camp came to the island to inquire about you, lad. Captain Peter told them that you were not here and after searching the island, they could see that for themselves. But I'm afraid they will be back. For your sake, too, we must leave at once."

"It will be wiser to wait until night when the guards at the fort can't see us," Captain Peter advised. "Just before the sun rises is the darkest time. Then many of the guards will be asleep at their posts."

"You're right, Captain Peter," agreed Christian Post. "We will leave just before sunrise."

How serene and peaceful the tall missionary was in the midst of danger, Peter thought. His faith in God's plan for him must be very strong. Had Peter's own parents accepted their fate so calmly? Was that the true Christian way?

As for himself, Peter was so excited that he tossed and turned under his rabbitskin robe most of the night. He was relieved when he felt a hand gently shaking his shoulder and he knew it was time to leave the island. Without a word Captain Peter motioned for the boys to get up. Hastily they rolled their robes and stole off with the others through the chestnut trees.

King Beaver's big dugout canoe was beached on the far side of the island. The Delaware king took his place in the bow and Captain Peter motioned for Christian Post and the boys to sit in the middle. Prisquetomen pushed the canoe offshore and without a sound the two guides began to paddle down the Allegheny and onto the Ohio.

Peter glanced back at the dark outline of Fort Duquesne standing on the point of land between two rivers, its stockade and bastions dark and sinister against the faint streaks of red and orange in the early morning sky. Somewhere behind those grim walls slept Sally Turner with her French family. Would he ever see her again, he wondered.

The dark river bluffs closed in on them as the current took the dugout farther down the Ohio. Now that they were a safe distance from the fort, Christian Post spoke for the first time. "I prayed that the Lord would blind them, as he did the enemies of Lot and Elijah, that we might pass unknown. The Lord heard my prayer."

No sooner had he spoken those words then they heard the cannon exploding many times from the fort. Peter glanced around with concern but Christian Post said, "The French always sound their great guns on the Sabbath."

The volleys echoed up the river canyons and Peter counted nineteen in all. He was glad when they rounded the big bend in the river and were out of sight from the fort.

The sun rose and the dark waters of the Ohio turned golden between the gray morning mists that clung to the black bluffs. Christian Post settled back to enjoy the journey.

"*La Belle Rivière*, the Beautiful River," he told Peter. "That's what the French call the Ohio."

Peter gazed over the broad crest of the great river, its deep green waters sparkling and peaceful. "It is pretty—and big," he said as he stared at the wide expanse of water ahead of them. "I never saw a river so big."

"It's the gateway to the west," Christian Post said.

"It leads to lands of the Ohio country unsettled by the white man."

"The Ohio is the land of the Delaware and the Shawnee," Captain Peter spoke up solemnly. "It remains as the Great Spirit made it."

And it was as God had made it, Peter thought as they drifted by heavily wooded banks of great sycamore, hickory, and oak. They floated past high cliffs with waterfalls leaping down over them. Fish jumped from dark pools along shore and grouse made sudden thunder with their wings back through the deep quiet woods.

Little Wolf pointed to a promontory of huge rocks where a bald eagle soared on the air currents, a free spirit let loose in this world of peace and beauty. The carefree Indian boy must have felt like the eagle, for he whistled a mixture of notes, announcing between whistles how happy he was to be away from the white man's fort and back in the Indian forest once more.

Many tributaries poured into the Ohio and at times several wooded islands rose up to cut the big river in two. At midday they stopped on one of these islands and ate some dried fish and leftover hoecake while the paddlers rested.

For the rest of the day the Delaware guides kept paddling steadily. The gentle motion of the big canoe and the warmth of the sun made Peter sleepy. He curled up in the bottom of the dugout and dozed.

The sun was sinking behind a cloud bank in the west when Peter awoke suddenly. The canoe was dipping and swaying in a strong crosscurrent. Peter peered ahead to see where they were and glimpsed the mouth of a small river that flowed into the Ohio from the north. Here the great river turned southward and they left it, going northwest up the smaller stream.

The paddlers dipped their blades deep into the swift current to make headway. Once they left the mouth of the river, the going was easier, even though they are still paddling upstream.

Now the river bluffs disappeared into gently rolling hills and on either side of the stream the shores leveled into rich bottomland. "It's as beautiful here along the little Beaver River as it is along the Ohio," Christian Post remarked. "I do love this western land, Peter."

At dusk they beached the dugout by an open meadow. On the far side of the glade Peter glimpsed a scattering of log houses and bark wigwams. "This is the Shawnee town of Sacunk," Little Wolf informed him. "We'll stay here for the night."

"Is it a friendly village?" asked Peter anxiously

The Delaware boy shrugged. "French Indians live here, but we'll be safe with King Beaver. He's respected by Shawnees and Delawares alike."

They walked across the meadow and just outside the village Prisquetomen called out a greeting. While they waited for his hallo to be answered, Christian Post gathered his traveling companions around him. He raised his hands to the darkened sky. "Let's pray," he said in English.

They knelt on the ground by their White Brother and Christian Post began his prayer. "O God, our Father, You have led us from the camp of our enemies so that we, Your servants, may continue to preach Your Word. Give us brave hearts and true understanding. Give us strength and courage to take our enemy by the hand and lead him to Your teachings. Let Your words of peace fall from our lips, and if persecuted, give us the heart to forgive, as our Savior forgave. Make Your will be our own. Amen."

Peter knew that the prayer was meant for him as much as for the loyal Delaware guides and he joined them in repeating "Amen."

Two men from the Shawnee village met them. When they saw King Beaver, they greeted him cordially and led him and his companions back to the Indian town. Mangy-looking dogs came running up, barking and snarling at the strangers. Half-dressed children peered out from behind door flaps. Warriors with painted faces stared at them, their eyes hard and narrow.

King Beaver was greeted in a friendly manner by the leaders, but when the Shawnee warriors saw the white missionary, they surrounded him with drawn knives in their hands.

Christian Post stood calmly before them, holding out his leather-bound Bible to show them that he was a man of God and carried no weapon. Peter supposed that the Shawnee warriors had never seen a Bible or book of any kind before. They drew back suspiciously, grunting and muttering to themselves as they pointed at the strange object in the white man's hands.

They looked in awe at this stranger who did not fear their knives. They watched solemnly as he opened the Bible and showed it to them.

Now as they gathered around the tall missionary

and looked in wonder at the strange black designs on the pages of the Book, they put aside their knives. Peter stared in fascination. It was as if God had just worked a miracle!

The Shawnee leaders led their guests to a large wigwam which Little Wolf told Peter must be their council lodge. Squaws brought roast venison and hominy. After the guests had eaten, the two chiefs of the village, Killbuck and Captain White Eyes, passed around a pipe and talked. Christian Post presented them with several strings of wampum and told them about Chief Teedyuscung's big hello.

The talk went on through the night and although the Shawnees now seemed friendly enough, Peter could not put the angry faces of the warriors out of his mind. He would be glad for daybreak. He was anxious to leave the Shawnee village of Sacunk and be on the way again.

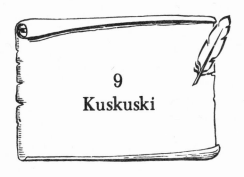

9

Kuskuski

"We'll soon be coming to Kuskuski," Christian Post told Peter the next day as the dugout made its way up the Beaver River. "It's a very important center for the Delaware clans. It's made up of four separate towns along this river. We're going to Old Kuskuski, the main town, where King Beaver lives. There I'm to meet with his brother, Shingas, and Delaware George, and the other Delaware captains."

Christian Post turned and smiled at Peter. "After the Delawares at Kuskuski hear Teedyuscung's big hello and I tell them about Governor Denny's offer of peace, we'll start eastward over the mountains. But that won't be tomorrow nor the next day. It takes patience to talk with Indians. Still, I'd as soon live among them as I would among white men."

To Peter these were surprising words. "Even after the way they treated you at Fort Duquesne and Sacunk?"

Christian Post nodded. "At Fort Duquesne and the Shawnee town I'm their enemy because they look upon me as English. At Kuskuski the Delawares know me, not as an Englishman, but as their Moravian brother. They know I would not fight against them in either the English or the French army. They know I come in peace."

It was dusk when they came to a wide bend in the river. A short distance from the bend the Beaver branched into two smaller streams. It was here in the forks that Peter glimpsed a village of bark wigwams, curling its smoke against the gray sky.

King Beaver went ahead to announce their arrival. When he returned, he had with him his brother, Shingas, and Delaware George. Like Beaver they wore fur robes over their shoulders and eagle feathers in their scalp locks. Their faces were grave and wrinkled with age.

"Brothers, our White Brother has come a great way and wants to see us at our council fire," King Beaver told them. "He brings with him a big hello from Teedyuscung, leader of our clans east of the great mountains, and a message from Governor Denny of Pennsylvania. He wants us to call the captains from all the towns. None should be missing."

Shingas stepped up to Christian Post. He held out

the palms of his hands in a greeting of friendship. "Brother, I am very glad to see you. I thank the Great Spirit who has brought you to us. Before another sun a runner will be sent to the towns of Kuskuski to spread the news that our White Brother wishes to talk with their chiefs. They will gather here to hear Teedyuscung's big hello.

"What my brother says pleases me," replied the tall missionary. "It's great that God has spared our lives to see one another again in love and friendship."

They went into the village. The scattering of log houses and wigwams in the open glade reminded Peter of the smaller Shawnee village of Sacunk. Dogs barked and a gathering of braves and squaws and children crowded around them as they made their way across the open space. But the faces of the squaws were friendly and the braves did not wear war paint nor did they carry knives.

The Delaware king led his visitors to a large lodge on the edge of the village. Later Peter learned that this lodge was especially built for strangers who were visiting Old Kuskuski. It reminded him of the big log house in Bethlehem that the brethren had built to entertain their Indian guests.

Prisquetomen started a fire in the fire pit and soon the cheery sound of crackling logs filled the room. The boys spread their robes on bunks of pine wood that lined the walls of the lodge. Wearily they sank down into mattresses of soft balsam boughs and fell asleep at once.

The next morning a soft rhythmic sound awakened Peter. *Ka-doom, ka-doom, ka-doom.*

It was the Indian women pounding corn in wooden

81

mortars. The boys arose early, eager to explore their new surroundings.

Kuskuski seemed to be a peaceful, friendly village. "It's different here from Sacunk and the camp at Fort Duquesne," Peter remarked as he and Little Wolf walked across the open space.

"That's because there are no Frenchmen or Englishmen living here," Little Wolf replied. "When the Delawares live with white men, they become lazy and noisy and quarrelsome. My father says it's because of the firewater the white men give them."

They found a footpath in back of the village and followed it through the woods. The trail led northward.

"If we kept following this trail we'd come to Fort Presque Isle on Lake Erie," Little Wolf said. "My father told me that all trails north of this town lead there." He stopped suddenly and put his finger to his mouth. "Someone's coming!"

He motioned quietly for Peter to slip behind a nearby tree.

"I don't hear anything," Peter whispered. "Why are we hiding like this?"

"Ottawas use this trail on their way to Fort Duquesne. They're the fierce French Indians from the Great Lakes and I wouldn't want to meet them without my father."

Peter heard a twig crack softly on the trail ahead. Then another and another. After several breathless moments, a man appeared through the trees. He was dressed in a long buckskin hunting shirt and Peter could tell that he was a chief by the cluster of eagle feathers twisted in his scalp lock. Several more chiefs followed. They were making their way down the trail to Old Kuskuski.

When they disappeared through the trees, Little Wolf slipped from his hiding place and grinned. "They're only Delaware captains coming to Old Kuskuski to hear our White Brother. Let's follow them back to the village."

When all the chiefs from the four villages of Kuskuski had arrived, King Beaver ordered the squaws to prepare a feast in honor of the White Brother's visit. Soon large kettles of succotash and potatoes were steaming over cooking fires and haunches of venison and rabbit were roasting on spits. Peter and Little Wolf stuffed themselves with the good food until they could eat no more. Then they took their places in the outer circle of squaws and children to watch the dancing which followed the feast.

A great pile of firewood was lighted in the open space. At the sound of the drum, one by one, the men and women circled the fire. Shuffling their feet and shaking turtle shell rattles, they chanted their monotonous dance song.

Hi-ho-ay-ah
Hi-ho-ay-ah

The bare shoulders of the braves gleamed like copper in the firelight. The long fringe on the shawls of the squaws swung back and forth gracefully to the rhythm of their swaying bodies. Into the circle of dancers leaped a large man wearing a grotesque mask of poplar wood and woodchuck hair. He fanned the fire with a fan of eagle's wings and threw fine tobacco into the flames. A thick sweet smoke filled the air.

Facing to the north and south, to the east and west, he chanted, "O, ho! O, ho! O, ho!"

"Who is he and what's he doing?" whispered Peter to Little Wolf.

"He's the medicine man. He's talking to the grandfathers and warriors of our people to the north and south, to the east and west. He is asking them to listen to the White Brother's messages with an open heart. It's a good sign for our White Brother's peace mission."

Peter was surprised that the feasting and dancing lasted several long days. Christian Post seemed to enjoy the celebration, but after the first day Peter grew restless. His head throbbed with the monotonous beat of the tom-toms and the endless chanting of the dancers. "Will they never stop celebrating?" he asked the missionary.

Christian Post smiled at the boy's anxious look. "Dancing and feasting puts them in a good mood, Peter. They do that before all their important council meetings. If white men would have such merriment before their serious decisions, I'm sure they'd go into their councils with a lighter heart, too."

"But we'll never get back over the mountains at this rate," protested Peter.

"Come, pray with me, lad. Let's ask the Lord for patience."

Peter knelt beside the missionary. After talking with the Lord, he was surprised how much better he felt. The Lord had given him patience to endure the waiting.

When at last the celebration ended, King Beaver summoned the chiefs and Christian Post to the council lodge. But before the chiefs listened to Teedyuscung's big hello, their spokesman arose and addressed the missionary.

"Brother, let me say this first. It is plain to see that you white people are the cause of this war. Why do the English and the French not fight in the old country or on the sea? Why do you come to fight on our land? This makes us believe you both want to take the land from us."

Christian Post replied, "Brothers, as for my part, I have not one foot of land, nor do I desire to have any. And if I had any land, I would rather give it to you than take it from you. But it is well that you keep nothing bitter in your hearts. I will take what you have said to the council fire at the Forks of the Delaware. I assure you that your words will be listened to."

The chiefs seemed satisfied and after Christian Post had read them Teedyuscung's big hello and the messages from the governor, King Beaver presented him with a white wampum belt with eight rows of beads.

"Brother," the Delaware king said, "your heart is good and you speak sincerely. We want you to have great courage and finish this peace which you have begun. When it is known among our brothers at the Forks of the Delaware and they everywhere agree upon it, then bring the great peace belt to us at Kuskuski. We'll send it to our brothers along the Ohio and when all here join in this friendship, the day will begin to shine clear over us. Now, brother, you know our hearts. Let the governor know of our thoughts with this belt."

Shingas added, "We want our White Brother to return to us as soon as the peace talks are finished so that our tribes may know of them. Then we can all live in peace as brothers again."

The missionary promised to return to Kuskuski.

Peter's heart sang. At last the long waiting was over. The Delawares of the Ohio had listened to Teedyuscung's big hello. Christian Post had accomplished his peace mission. Now he was free to return to the East and Peter would return with him.

No sooner had the council ended when a Mingo runner came to Old Kuskuski with disturbing news.

"Captain de Ligneris is angry that the White Brother has escaped from the island in the Allegheny. He has set a great price on the White Brother's head," the Mingo said. "He is sending scouts out to wait for the White Brother on the trails leading over the mountains. Our father, the French, wants them to deliver the White Brother to the fort as a prisoner, or to bring back his scalp. I know the trails where his scouts will be waiting and I will guide our White Brother across the mountains a safer way. But we must leave at once."

Christian Post at once prepared to leave. Prisquetomen filled the food bags with dried venison and corn. Captain Peter brought the horses from the corral and saddled them. Peter and Little Wolf hurried about rolling the sleeping robes into tight bundles.

When at last they were assembled in the open space, King Beaver and Shingas drew the missionary aside and spoke to him in grave tones. Christian Post answered them with equally grave tones. Several times he shook his head.

Eager to be off, Peter shifted impatiently from one foot to the other. What were they talking about so earnestly? Why were they delaying so long when danger lay ahead of them? Peter felt suddenly uneasy when they turned now and then to look at him.

The Delawares stopped talking and folded their arms across their chests. They stared in stony silence. Finally Christian Post came to where Peter was standing and spoke to him. There was great sadness on his face.

"Peter, King Beaver and Shingas want you to stay here at Old Kuskuski until I return with news of the peace talks at the Forks of the Delaware. They say you are the rightful prisoner of the Delawares and not until the treaty of peace has been signed can Delaware prisoners be freed."

Peter's heart froze. "But—but—can't you do *something?*" he cried in a choked voice.

Christian Post shook his head sadly. "I have tried to talk them into letting you go but they refuse. You see, lad, it's a matter of principle that you stay here until the treaty is signed. It's their custom."

Peter felt hot tears welling up into his eyes. So he wasn't free after all! He was still a captive! He tried to choke back the tears but they burned on his cheeks.

The missionary put his hand on the boy's arm. "My heart is as sad as yours, Peter. All I can do is to pray that I can return as soon as possible to Kuskuski. It is now the eighth of September by my almanac. God willing, by November, before the big snows, I should be here again. Until then the Delawares in Kuskuski will treat you as their own son, and my faithful guide, Captain Peter, and his son, Little Wolf, have offered

87

to remain here with you. You will be safe in their lodge."

Peter bit his lip and turned away. Christian Post's voice echoed behind him.

"The Lord challenges us to do His will, Peter. He shapes our destinies as He wills. At times we cannot understand but we must be patient. If we trust in the Lord, then He will keep us in perfect peace."

Peter was angry and puzzled over the missionary's words. Why did Christian Post have to talk about God's will and his destiny all the time? What destiny would he have here in this Indian village so far from his home?

"God doen't care what happens to me!" he burst out bitterly.

The missionary walked to his saddlebag. He took the leather-bound Bible and held it out to Peter.

"I know the brethren at Bethlehem have taught you to read, Peter. God's Word will give you the strength you need until I return. Whenever your faith in Him wavers or whenever you are frightened or discouraged, read His Book and it will comfort you."

Peter stared at the Bible. "But you may need it more than I!"

Christian Post shook his head. "Take it, lad. It is *you* who needs it more."

Peter's trembling hands touched the Bible. He held it close to him as the tall missionary mounted his horse and rode off.

Little Wolf came to stand by his side. He put his hand on the white boy's shoulder. Together they watched the forest beyond the river long after Christian Post and his guides had disappeared.

Peter was angry and puzzled. Why did Christian Post have to talk about God's will all the time?

10
The Wood-Carver's Lodge

Peter was running for his life. Faster and faster he ran but the ugly painted faces, the clubs and switches kept whirling around his head. A leather-bound Bible was thrust in front of him. He grasped it, but a soldier in a blue coat reached out, tugging at it, trying to take it away. Peter hung onto the Book for dear life but he felt it slipping from his grasp. Slipping—slipping— Then all went black and he cried out in anguish.

He opened his eyes and sat up with a start. He was wet with cold sweat and his hand ached as it tightly grasped the leather-bound Bible.

How many nights had he had this same dream!

Would it never go away, Peter wondered.

He stared into the dimness of the lodge at the huddled forms of Captain Peter and Little Wolf lying in bunks across from his. Their quiet shapes were reassuring and he sank back in his own bunk exhausted. He tossed and turned. Sleep never came easily after that nightmare.

He tried to think of other things. He thought about Christian Post asleep somewhere along a hidden trail in the Endless Mountains. Would the brave missionary be able to escape his pursuers or would he be captured and made a prisoner in the French fort? Worse yet, would he be killed and his scalp returned to Captain de Ligneris?

Peter blinked as he watched the glowing embers in the fire pit. He feared for the missionary's safety but at the same time marveled at his faith. It was the same faith his parents must have had when they had preached to the Indians at Gnadenhuetten. Peter wished he had some of that faith now.

He glanced down at the Bible he was still holding tightly. Gradually his fingers relaxed and he opened it to a place that had been marked with a slender twig. By the vague glow of the embers he scanned the pages until his eyes came to the words, "When I am afraid, I put my trust in Thee."

He read the passage over and over until a calmness settled over him and he dropped off to a more peaceful sleep.

The next morning the smell of frying corn bread awakened Peter. Little Wolf and his father were already up. They were waiting for him by the fire.

"Our White Brother always starts the day reading the Great Spirit's words," Captain Peter said.

Peter handed him the Bible but the Indian captain shook his head. "Our little brother will read them to us now."

Peter remembered that in Bethlehem Brother Joseph had always read the Lord's Prayer at the beginning of each new day. He opened the Bible to the familiar place, Matthew, chapter six. His voice shook a little but he read reverently. When he finished, the Indian father seemed satisfied and handed him a bowl of corn bread and fish.

After breakfast Little Wolf came to sit next to Peter. He was knotting some threadlike spruce roots into a long line. At the end of the line he tied a tiny sharp bird bone.

"Today my brother and I will go fishing," he said. "We will have a good supper of fried fish tonight."

Peter's spirits rose. He would be glad to leave the smoky lodge and be alone in the forest with Little Wolf.

On their way across the glade, they passed some boys who were shooting mark with bows and arrows. Little Wolf paused to watch. His eyes shone as he looked back at the shooting match.

"Watch! I will show them how to hit the mark," he cried. Eager to show off his skill, he ran to join them.

Peter sat on a stump to watch. Each boy took a turn at trying to hit a bear's paw that was tied to the stout trunk of a hickory tree. When it was Little Wolf's turn, he stepped up to the target and notched an arrow to the bowstring. He pulled back expertly on the bowstring and sent the arrow singing through the air.

It found its mark right in the center of the paw.

The boys shouted and rallied around the Delaware boy. Then one of them turned and pointed to Peter. Before Peter realized what was happening, the Indian boys came running across the glade toward him. They thrust the bow into his hands and pointed to the bear's paw.

Peter was about to turn and run when Little Wolf said, "If you don't try, my brother, they'll think you are a coward."

Peter walked slowly to the hickory tree. He fitted an arrow to the bowstring. He clutched the bow with his good hand but he could not pull back on the bowstring with his crooked fingers. The boys laughed as they watched the white boy struggle with the bow. But when they saw his crippled hand for the first time, they stopped laughing and just stared.

With disgust Peter threw the bow to the ground and ran for the woods. He was hoping they wouldn't follow, but he knew they were coming by the quick moccasined steps behind him.

He would show these Indian boys how fast a boy with crooked fingers could run! He sped ahead and they quickened their pace, trying to catch him. He gritted his teeth and ran as fast as he could across the glade. Just before he dashed into the woods, he turned. They had fallen behind but he glimpsed a new look of admiration on the face of the boy in the lead. He had outrun them all and they knew they couldn't catch him.

Peter kept running through the woods until he came to the river. He flung himself down on the bank, panting. He looked at his withered hand then quickly hid it from his sight. What could God's plan be for him when He gave him twisted fingers, Peter wondered bitterly.

For a long while he sat along the riverbank, idly watching the fish jump. He did not hear the soft moccasined footsteps approaching. Not until a voice spoke behind him did he whirl around and see a girl standing there.

She was dressed in a deerskin tunic which hung down over fringed leggings. Her dark straight hair was held back by a beaded headband. She did not smile but her eyes were friendly. She held out her hand and Peter stared at what she was holding. It was the wooden lamb his father had carved for him.

He took the lamb and turned questioning eyes to the girl. With gestures she pointed back toward the meadow. The carving must have fallen from his waistcloth as he was running away from the Indian boys.

The girl looked at the wooden lamb and said words Peter did not understand. She pointed to the carving and then to him.

In a sudden flash of understanding, Peter realized that she was trying to ask him if he had carved it. He shook his head.

Still staring at the carving, she looked puzzled. Peter doubted that she had ever seen a real lamb before.

"Lamb," he said, pointing to the carving and trying to make her understand.

She laughed at the strange-sounding word then pulled his arm as if she wanted him to follow her. Peter shook his head but she kept pulling at him until he finally gave in and followed.

She led the way to a lodge on the edge of the woods where an old man was sitting on a rush mat by the door flap. He was busy carving a bowl out of a chunk of soft basswood.

The girl said a few words in Delaware to the old man then motioned for Peter to show him the carved lamb. The Indian reached out his gnarled old fingers to touch the smooth wood. His eyes brightened with admiration as he examined the carving. Then he got up stiffly and motioned for Peter and the girl to follow him into his lodge.

Peter looked around curiously. The inside of the lodge was like a workshop. Wooden shelves filled with spoons, ladles, bowls, and stirring sticks—all carved out of wood, lined the cedar bark walls. The girl led Peter to a shelf with all kinds of carved animals and birds on it. Peter examined one of the carvings closely. It was a beautifully carved rabbit with sharp pointed ears and even a round fluff of a tail. Why, it was as well carved as his father's lamb!

"*Muschgingus*," the girl said as she pointed to the wooden rabbit.

"*Muschgingus*," Peter repeated. Then he held out his father's carving. "Lamb," he said again. This time the Indian girl giggled and repeated the word slowly.

Peter pointed to himself.

"Peter," he said.

Pointing to herself, the girl replied, "Tschimalus."

She laughed when Peter stumbled over her long name. She pointed to the old wood-carver and called him *Muchomes*.

Peter learned that the bowl Muchomes was carving

was called *walacans* and that wood was *tachan.* Learning the Delaware names for the different objects in the wood-carver's lodge was like playing a game and before he knew it, Peter was speaking words in the Delaware language.

After that day Peter often visited Muchomes' lodge. He liked to sit and watch the old man carve. He learned that Tschimalus, whose name meant bluebird in English, was his granddaughter.

Every time Peter came to the wood-carver's lodge, Bluebird would teach him more Delaware words. One day while she was looking at his carved lamb, Peter was able to make her understand that his father had carved it.

"He carves as well as Grandfather," Bluebird said. "Do you carve in wood, too, like your father?"

Peter shook his head and glanced down at his crippled hand.

"I can't," he said.

Bluebird did not seem to understand. She picked up a block of basswood from her grandfather's shelf and handed it to him.

"Carve me a lamb like your father's, Peter."

Peter quickly hid his crippled hand behind him. His ears burned with shame. Was she, too, making fun of him?

But Bluebird's eyes were not mocking him; they were serious. They were begging him to try.

Muchomes handed Peter a cutting tool. "The knife and the wood are yours," he said.

For a long time Peter stared at the knife and the piece of wood. Had Bluebird and her grandfather really thought that he could learn to carve like his father? Slowly he picked up the knife. It felt awkward in his hand. He took a firmer grip on it. Holding the block of basswood firmly against his chest with his twisted fingers, he started shaving off tiny chips of wood.

Muchomes showed him how to make a pattern of the lamb to put on the block of wood, then Peter set to work in earnest while Bluebird's watching eyes encouraged him. Before long the knife did not feel so awkward in his hand and the crude carving began to take shape.

As the days passed Peter looked forward to his visits with Bluebird and her grandfather. He looked upon them as his friends, encouraging and helping him to do the thing he had always wanted to do but thought he never could do. No longer did he hide his crippled hand behind his back in their lodge. He needed it to hold the wood he was carving.

One day as he was leaving for the wood-carver's lodge, Little Wolf called to him.

"I am going into the forest to set some snares. Would my brother like to come along?"

Peter hesitated. It was a bright blue day and the forest did look inviting. It was a long time since he had been out of the Indian village. Peter gladly joined Little Wolf.

As they walked along the riverbank, Peter noticed that the Virginia creeper had turned crimson on the tree trunks and the maples were dropping their red and yellow leaves. A flock of honking geese made long irregular wedges southward over the treetops. September must be over, Peter thought; it must be well into October.

On their way through the forest, he asked Little Wolf the Delaware names of the things they passed. *"Hittuk,"* Little Wolf said when Peter pointed to a tree. The dead flower that grew under the tree was a *woatawes*. The rock next to the flower was a *pemapuchk* and the sky above it was *pemapanik*.

Little Wolf pointed to a deer browsing in a clearing and said, *"Achtu."* Then pointing to Peter and smiling, he said, *"Kschamehhellan."*

"That is the name the boys in the village have given you, my brother. It means He-who-runs-like-the-wind."

Peter smiled back. He liked the sound of his Indian name.

They set the first snare for muskrat along the river-bank. Peter held the snare while Little Wolf tied the slip noose to a low branch. Farther back in the forest they set fox and rabbit snares. Toward the end of the day the shelter of a pine woods drew them in. The boys piled a mound of soft pine needles on the ground for their bed and spread Little Wolf's robe over it for a covering.

"We do not need a lean-to in this grove," the Indian boy said, pointing up at the pine branches that covered them like a thick green roof.

They had found a plump rabbit in one of the snares and roasted the loin and legs on green sticks over a campfire. That night under the sheltering pines they lay like the quiet deer, breathing the same fragrant air and listening to the same quiet murmur of the wind among the trees. The moon showed its full face, cold and bright. The night air had a touch of frost in it. They lay close to each other for warmth.

They passed the next day like happy animals, wandering through colored woods and sunlit glades, their own masters. Peter began to understand Little Wolf's love for this beautiful, primitive land. As he followed his friend's footsteps over leafy traces that only the deer had made, he too felt a great feeling of contentment.

The past was behind him; only this day that lay ahead mattered. Like his Indian brother he began to think of the sun as his father and the earth as his mother and the creatures of the forest as his brothers and sisters. The white man's world seemed far away.

For several days they wandered through the forest, checking their snares, fishing in the river when they cared to, and living off the land. Little Wolf seemed to be in no hurry to return to the village and Peter shared this feeling. Only a change in the weather stopped their carefree wanderings. Little Wolf could hear the storm approach before it reached them. The restless wind in the treetops and the moaning of the pines told him that it was time to return to the village.

The east wind was blowing rain in their faces by the time they came out of the forest. They raced each other across the glade and through the village. Flinging back the door flap of their lodge, they stopped short and stared in surprise.

Two French soldiers in blue coats and black tricornered hats were seated with Captain Peter and the Delaware king by the fire pit. And next to them was a French Indian, his back turned to the boys.

When Peter saw the Indian, he tensed. What were he and the Frenchmen doing in their guest lodge? Peter wondered. Then a sudden anxious thought came to him. Could the Indian be the one who had captured him before? Had he come to Kuskuski with the soldiers to hunt for Peter? Had he come to claim his white captive and take him back to Fort Duquesne?

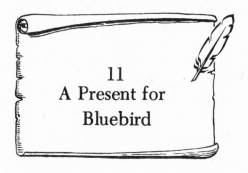

11
A Present for
Bluebird

Panic rose inside Peter as he stared at the little group of men around the fire. He was about to back away and run for his life when Little Wolf reached out and seized his arm.

"I know what my brother is thinking," Little Wolf said in a guarded voice, "but that brave is not a Delaware. He is an Ottawa from the Great Lakes. I can tell by his headdress."

The boys stood quietly and listened to the men who were jabbering together in a mixture of Delaware and French so that all could understand.

"They must have come from Fort Duquesne," Little Wolf said in a low voice. "I wonder what they're doing here?"

He listened closely. A few moments later he whispered to Peter, "The French captain wants the young chiefs and braves of Kuskuski to meet with Captain de Ligneris at the fort."

Peter's thoughts whirled. What would the commandant want with the men of Kuskuski? Whatever it was, Peter felt sure it concerned the fate of Christian Post.

The talk went on for most of the night and Peter was lulled to sleep by the droning of voices around the fire. When he awoke the next morning, the lodge was empty except for Little Wolf.

"Where has everyone gone?" Peter asked. "Where is your father?"

"My father went along with the chiefs and braves to Fort Duquesne to find out what the commandant wants with them."

"But won't he be in danger because he helped Christian Post escape?"

"My father is a chief," Little Wolf said proudly. "Captain de Ligneris would not dare to harm a chief of the Delawares."

"What Captain de Ligneris wants with the men from Kuskuski must be very important," Peter remarked as he listened to the rain drumming on the roof of the lodge. "They didn't even wait for the storm to pass."

Little Wolf nodded a silent agreement and frowned thoughtfully into the fire.

The rain continued for several days. Peter spent most of the time in Muchomes' wigwam, finishing the carving of the lamb. When it was done, he was pleased and surprised to find that it was almost as good as the lamb his father had carved.

Muchomes nodded with satisfaction as he examined it and Peter was thrilled with the old man's look of praise.

After he had polished the wood so that it was smooth and shiny, Peter gave the carving to Bluebird. Her face shone as she held it in her hand.

"Lamb," she said softly in English.

In return she brought out a gift she had made for Peter. It was a warm, buckskin-fringed hunting jacket, with the emblem of the wolf clan embroidered with beadwork on the front of it.

"When the snow moon comes, Peter will not have to walk around with his robe draped over him, looking like a big brown rabbit," she told him laughing.

Peter put on the new jacket. How soft and warm the leather felt against his skin! He was so grateful for Bluebird's gift that he wanted to carve something else for her. But he couldn't decide what it would be. Muchomes' shelves were filled with carvings of animals and birds and fish. But Peter wanted his next carving to be something different.

It was on another stormy day that an idea came to him. As Peter sat close to the fire and watched the first big flakes of wet snow drift down through the smoke hole and sizzle on the hot stones of the fire pit, they reminded him of his home in Bethlehem. After the first autumn snow, the Moravian children would go into the woods to gather moss and evergreens for the Christmas putz, or manger scene, that was to be set up in the chapel. What fun it had been to help the

103

brethren and sisters make the manger scene!

The moss would be put on the floor as a thick, green carpet for the carved figures of Joseph and Mary and the Christ Child. Some of the brethren had even carved the three wise men and the shepherds with their sheep to place in the putz with the Holy Family. And around the entire manger scene would be the fragrance of the evergreens.

As Peter thought of this happy time of year, he knew what he could carve for Bluebird that would be different from anything Muchomes had made.

"I will carve Joseph, Mary, and the Christ Child," he spoke his thoughts aloud to Little Wolf. "I will gather moss and pine boughs from the forest to put with the carved figures, just as they do in Bethlehem!" He could hardly wait to get started with his idea.

"I will show my brother where the pine and the basswood grow," Little Wolf said, eager for an excuse to go into the forest again. "We will gather moss along the banks of the river."

The snow had melted by the time the boys started for the forest but the sky was still filled with cold gray clouds. Little Wolf led the way to a grove of linden trees. Nearby were some thick pines. When Peter had found the right kind of wood to carve his three figures, they started back toward the riverbank. They were coming out on the trail when through the leafless trees they saw a man coming toward them. Little Wolf watched the man closely.

"My father!" he cried, and with a whoop of joy, he ran to meet the chief.

At the lodge Captain Peter took off his stiff, muddy

moccasins and warmed his feet by the fire while the boys dished out bowls of steaming stew.

"Rabbit stew lies well on the tongue," Captain Peter said after he had finished eating. "For many suns I have been away. It is good to be back again to this lodge."

"My father returns alone," said Little Wolf, puzzled.

Captain Peter nodded. "The young chiefs and braves have stayed to join the raiding parties of French soldiers. Their minds have been dulled by the lies the French father tells them."

"Lies?" echoed the boys in one voice.

Captain Peter's face was grim. "Captain de Ligneris told them that the English soldiers are marching over the mountains to destroy the Delawares, the Shawnees, and the Mingoes. He said that our White Brother speaks with a forked tongue. He told the chiefs and warriors that the talks of peace are lies to get the Indians to lay down their tomahawks so that the English can destroy them. The commandant says that there is no peace council at the Forks of the Delaware."

"Our White Brother does not tell English lies," Little Wolf spoke up angrily. "He wants our brothers to stop fighting for their own good. When he returns with the peace treaty between Chief Teedyuscung and the English, he will prove that the French father is wrong!"

"Our White Brother's return to Kuskuski may be dangerous, my son, now that Captain de Ligneris has filled our brothers' bodies with firewater and their minds with doubt and hate. The French father has promised a rich reward if the Delaware braves bring our White Brother to Fort Duquesne as a prisoner when he returns to Kuskuski."

As he listened to the chief's words, Peter feared more than ever for the safe return of the missionary. But he remembered what Christian Post had told him that sleepless night on the island in the Allegheny.

"My life is in God's hands, Peter. He will do with it as He wills. It is not we who are important; it is why we were placed on this earth that is important. We all have a destiny and we must accept God's will."

"It must be faith in God that gives our White Brother the courage to face such dangers," Peter said aloud. "It must be a wonderful thing to have such faith!"

"Faith *is* a wonderful thing, my son," said Captain Peter. It was the first time he had referred to the white boy as his son and at that moment Peter felt very close to the Delaware chief.

From that day on Peter and Little Wolf began to watch the trails for Christian Post's return. "If only we knew where he is and that he is safe!" Peter would exclaim as he glanced into the dark empty forest.

It was one cold November afternoon that the missionary returned to the Delaware village. His faithful guide, Prisquetomen, was with him. Christian Post was as happy to find Peter safe and in good spirits as the boy was to see him alive and well.

"Why, lad," he told Peter when he arrived at the lodge, "you have grown since I left." He glanced at the wooden figure on Peter's bunk. "What is this you are carving?"

Peter told how Muchomes had taught him to carve.

He told about the manger scene he was making for Bluebird. "This is Joseph," he said handing Christian Post the wooden figure he had almost finished.

"I knew you would make good use of your hands someday," Christian Post said, observing the carving closely. "God does not give us afflictions so great that we cannot overcome them. You have your father's natural ability to be a good wood-carver."

Captain Peter and King Beaver greeted their White Brother warmly. "It is good that the Great Spirit has sent you back to us safe and well," the Delaware king said.

"I have brought with me good news," Christian Post told them all. "In my saddlebags is a copy of the treaty of peace with the English which Teedyuscung and the Six Nations have signed at the Forks of the Delaware. There are also letters from Governor Denny and General Forbes containing words of friendship and peace. Now that the treaty is made, we must read it to our brothers so that they can lay down their tomahawks and return to their villages in peace."

"Our news is not so good," Captain Peter said. "The young chiefs and braves of Kuskuski are with the French at Fort Duquesne. Our White Brother's life may be in danger when they return."

The missionary accepted the disturbing news with his usual calmness.

"We are here again to talk peace with our brothers, the Ohio Indians, to turn them from their warlike ways," he replied with confidence. "I know God will grant us His grace whereby we can do it."

Then Christian Post told them about his journey

across the mountains. "Governor Denny wanted me to inform General Forbes about the Indian treaty on my way to Kuskuski so we traveled west over the new military road."

"It was good you did not take the trails across the mountains," Captain Peter said. "They are being watched by French scouts."

"Where are the general and his army camped?" King Beaver wanted to know.

"The general's camp is at the new fort, Ligonier, on Chestnut Ridge, fifty miles from the Forks of the Ohio. The march across the mountains was slow because the general took sick with a stomach ailment and had to be carried from Raystown to Fort Ligonier on a litter slung between two horses."

King Beaver turned strickened eyes upon the missionary. "A sick general marching against Fort Duquesne! He will be cut down as quickly as Braddock before him."

"The new English chief is a much wiser man than Braddock," Christian Post assured him. "His soldiers call him Head of Iron. He is determined to march to Fort Duquesne even though he has to be carried there on a litter. He will see that the lands of the Ohio are freed from the wars and bloodshed of the French."

The missionary turned to Peter and Little Wolf. "I left my saddlebags on my horse. They are heavy with letters and peace belts. Will you please bring them in?"

The two boys hurried from the lodge and found Christian Post's brown horse hobbled in the corral just outside the village. They unfastened the leather straps which held the saddlebags in place. Just as they were lifting the heavy bags from the horse, Little Wolf gasped, "Look!"

Then Peter, too, glimpsed the French captain with four solders riding out of the woods. The next moment a hair-raising scalp hallo burst from the throats of their Indian guides.

"Hurry!" Little Wolf cried. "If they see these saddlebags, they will know that our White Brother has returned. Come, we've got to warn him."

The boys ran quickly back to the village, the heavy saddlebags bumping against their legs. They slid through the door flap and blurted out breathlessly, "Five Frenchmen and some Indians are coming to Kuskuski!"

Prisquetomen made a quick movement toward the entrance. "Did they see you?"

"I don't think so," Peter replied.

The Delaware guide turned the edge of the door flap back and peered out. "I don't see them" he said. "They must not have entered the village yet."

"Captain de Ligneris has promised our brothers a rich reward if they bring the White Brother to the fort as a prisoner," King Beaver warned the missionary. "They may have come to look for you in Kuskuski. It will be well for my White Brother not to go far from this lodge."

Christian Post smiled at his worried friends. "Don't fear," he told them. "As God had stopped the mouths of the lions so that they could not devour Daniel, so He will preserve me from their fury and bring me through."

12
A Message for the
General

King Beaver went out to meet the French captain and his men. When he returned, he reported, "They are part of a scouting party who had a skirmish with some English soldiers within twelve miles of Fort Duquesne. The captain boasts that they killed an English lieutenant, four of his men, and took five more prisoners."

Christian Post shook his head sadly. "The English lieutenant must have been Lieutenant Hays, whom General Forbes sent to guide us from Fort Ligonier to the Ohio River. On his return to Fort Ligonier, he must have been ambushed by the French scouting party. Where did they take the prisoners?"

"They took them to Sacunk," Beaver replied. "One of the prisoners is to be burned at the stake."

Forgetting his own safety, Christian Post arose from the fire pit. "I must meet with the scouting party at once. Give me the Bible, Peter. I shall surely need it now."

Peter got the leather-bound Bible. With it tucked under his arm, Christian Post left the lodge.

Some of the warriors in the scouting party were Delawares from Old Kuskuski. When they saw the missionary, they said, "Brother, we did not know the lieutenant and his men were your escorts. We are sorry it has happened."

"What is done is done, my brothers," Christian Post replied, "but sadness has come to my heart that you did not have faith in my peace talks."

"The French father has given us bad medicine," one of the Delawares admitted shamefully.

"Then let us take good medicine," said Christian Post, opening his Bible.

A hush settled over the gathering as he read, "God shall judge between nations, and shall decide for many peoples; and they shall beat their swords into plowshares, and their spears into pruning hooks; nation shall not lift up sword against nation, neither shall they learn war any more."

He closed the Bible and looked with flashing blue eyes at the circle of Delawares. "Let us follow God's Word and undo the wrongs to those who are prisoners at Sacunk. Let us relieve them from their misery. What messenger will go to Sacunk where the prisoner is to be burned and ask the Shawnees to spare him that terrible fate?"

At this request the scouts drew back, murmuring among themselves. Finally one of them ventured forward and offered to go.

"*Non! Non!*" cried the French captain.

But the Delaware turned his head, ignoring the officer. King Beaver rewarded the messenger with five hundred black wampum and Christian Post sent with him a peace belt by which he was to tell the Shawnees about the treaty at the Forks of the Delaware and about their White Brother's arrival at Old Kuskuski.

"Accompany him to Sacunk," Christian Post told Prisquetomen. "Then go on to Fort Ligonier and inform the general about the fate of Lieutenant Hays and his escorts."

Not long after Prisquetomen and the messenger had left Kuskuski, the chiefs and the rest of the warriors returned from Fort Duquesne. The younger braves gave the war hallo as they entered the village. They were painted with war paint and carried guns and spears.

"The young men still have war and hatred in their hearts from the raids Captain de Ligneris has sent them on," Captain Peter observed. "Our White Brother had best stay in the lodge until their rage passes."

"They are coming to the lodge now!" cried Little Wolf, who had been watching from the door flap.

"Have good courage and be strong," Christian Post told them quietly. Then as if in prayer, he lifted his eyes upward and murmured, " 'I will say of the Lord, He is my refuge and my fortress: my God; in him will I trust.' "

No sooner had the missionary uttered those words then the door flap was flung aside and the leader of the warriors stepped into the lodge. Peter drew back in horror when he saw the chief's fearful-looking face. Loops of a snake were painted in black across his forehead and down the side of one cheek. Two lances crossing each other were tattooed on the other cheek. His black eyes flashed with quick anger as he pointed to the White Brother.

"One that has but half an eye can see that the English mean to destroy us," he challenged the tall missionary. "Our White Brother speaks with a forked tongue. His talks of peace are lies to get his brothers to lay down their tomahawks so that the English can destroy the French and then destroy us!"

King Beaver stepped up to the gathering of angry young men. He pushed the leader aside. "I am ashamed to hear such talk from you," he said. "You are but a boy who has been given bad medicine by our father, the French. Give our White Brother his chance to speak. When you have heard what he has to say, you will become a man again."

The young chief looked scornfully at the old king, but he drew back to let the White Brother speak. The French soldiers with their captain lingered like dark shadows behind the warriors.

Christian Post opened his saddlebags and held up a large white belt with the figure of a man at each end and streaks of black representing the road from Philadelphia to the Ohio. The belt was from the governor of Pennsylvania.

"Brothers, I see that your bodies are stained with blood and I see anger in your eyes. With this belt of wampum I clean your bodies from blood and anoint your eyes with healing oil so that you may see your true brothers clearly. May the road be open between us."

Then Christian Post told them about the peace treaty that was made at the Forks of the Delaware between Teedyuscung and their uncles, the Six Indian Nations, and the English. He held up a copy of the treaty for all to see.

A murmur ran through the gathering like the hum of a rising storm, then faded away as Christian Post raised his hands to speak again.

"In his letter to the Delawares, the Shawnees, and the Mingoes on the Ohio, General Forbes writes that he is happy that all past disputes between the Indian Nations and the English have been settled at the Forks of the Delaware. He assures his brothers that his army is not coming to the Ohio to harm them but only to stop the bloodshed and war. With this belt of wampum the general assures his brothers that there shall be peace between the English and all the Indian nations from the rising sun to the setting sun."

The Delaware king took the belts Christian Post handed him and Shingas said, "Brother, now that we have seen the peace treaty with our own eyes and have heard the words of the general, we believe your words are good. We will give these belts to all the towns and tribes as you desired us."

Christian Post brought out a peace pipe sent by the Society of Friends of Philadelphia. The Delaware kings lighted it and passed it among the chiefs and warriors. As they smoked the peace pipe, Peter noticed that the anger had left the faces of the young warriors and soon they began to laugh and talk among themselves.

King Beaver spoke again. "Take notice, all you young men, to what we answer now. The treaty of peace between our brothers, the English, and our uncles, the Six Nations, has come to pass. Our uncles have made peace with our brothers, the English, and they have shaken hands with them. We likewise will agree in peace and friendship and will have peace with them."

Turning to the French captain, Shingas said, "Our White Brother wants us to do what is good and right, but since your warriors came among us, we could not follow what is good and right. Now with the help of our White Brother we will try again to do what is good and not let ourselves be disturbed any more by your warriors."

The French captain turned to the young chiefs. His lips were smiling but his cold gray eyes were hard. "My children," he said, "have you forgotten what your father, the French, has told you? The English are coming with an army to destroy both you and me. I desire you at once, my children, to hasten with all the young men. We will drive the English away and destroy them. The French father will tell you always what is best."

The captain laid a string of wampum before the chiefs. Peter tensed. What would happen now? Would the Delaware chiefs accept the French wampum?

But their leader turned to the French captain and said, "I have just heard something from our White Brother which pleases me better. I will not go! Give it to the others; maybe they will go."

The French captain took up the string of beads and said, jokingly, "He will not go! He has listened to the English lies!"

Then all the young chiefs cried out, "Yes, yes! We will listen to our White Brother."

His eyes flashing with anger, the French captain threw the string of wampum to where the warriors stood. But the young men kicked the string from one to another as if it were a snake. Captain Peter took a stick and with it flung the wampum belt from one end of the room to another.

"Give it back to the French captain and let him go with his young men," he said angrily.

Little Wolf gazed at his father with awe. "I have never seen my father so angry," he told Peter.

The face of the French captain went pale. He snatched up the string and without ceremony stalked from the lodge. Captain Peter followed him. When he returned, he said, "The Frenchmen are leaving for Fort Duquesne. Now the commandant will know how we at Kuskuski stand!"

To celebrate the peace treaty, the Delawares threw aside their weapons and for many days they danced and feasted. This time Peter and Little Wolf did not sit in the outer circle to watch. They joined in the festivities and danced around the ceremonial fire with the other Indian boys. On the last day of the celebration, Christian Post called Peter to his side.

"Prisquetomen has sent a message that General Forbes and his army have left Fort Ligonier, Peter. They are marching toward the Forks of the Ohio and are camped at a place called Turtle Creek, a day's march from Fort Duquesne. I am sending my faithful guide, Captain Peter, to the general's camp with the good news of the Delawares accepting the treaty of peace. It is necessary that General Forbes knows how the Delawares stand before he reaches the French fort, for it might help prevent unnecessary bloodshed."

He showed Peter the letter, folded and sealed with wax, that he had written to the general. "According to the treaty at the Forks of the Delaware, all English captives are to be set free, Peter; so it is safe now for you to leave Kuskuski. I have written to the general about you, and when you reach the English camp with Captain Peter, he will see that you get back to Path Valley."

Peter looked up at the missionary with surprise. "But, sir, what about you? I thought we would be going back East together now that your mission here is done."

Christian Post shook his head. "Ah, but my mission here is not done, Peter. It is just beginning. If the general and his men are successful in ridding the Forks of the Ohio of the French, Governor Denny has promised the Delawares, the Shawnees, and the Mingoes that no white man will settle in the rich hunting grounds beyond the rivers. The Ohio lands will remain the home of the Indians. I hope to go there with my Delaware brothers and start a mission. The chiefs have asked me to teach them God's Word in return for the promise to lay down their tomahawks."

The rough features of the missionary softened. "You see, lad, it is God's will—and my destiny. I must fulfill God's plan for me just as your father and mother fulfilled theirs."

"But sir," Peter protested, "look what the savages did to my father and mother at their mission. The Delawares might become angry again and do the same thing to you!"

The missionary's face saddened. "The Delawares were not always savages, Peter. Before the white man came to their lands, they were the gentle children of the forest. But the white man stole their lands and gave them rum in return. Both the French and the English taught them to hate and kill. Where hatred is bred, there is nothing too mean for men to do."

Christian Post paused and looked steadily at Peter. "Surely you have found kindness here in Kuskuski."

Peter nodded. "Captain Peter and Little Wolf and Bluebird and her grandfather have been good to me. Will you be staying with them?"

"I will be with all my friends here," the missionary replied. "Haven't I told you, lad, that I would as soon live with my brothers here in the wilderness than in the white towns of the East?"

He went on to explain. "White people have a weakness of wanting more and more. They pen themselves up in forts and towns where their greed cannot escape. The Indians have the freedom of the forest. It makes them feel akin to all God's creatures and they want to share the wonders of the earth with them. That is why, Peter, I prefer the Indian way of life."

Remembering the happy, carefree days he and Little Wolf had spent together in the forest, Peter understood what the missionary meant.

"Captain Peter is ready to leave so this is good-bye, lad," Christian Post said. "I hope, if God wills, that we shall meet again."

Peter stooped to fold his robe then he followed the missionary to the corral where Little Wolf was standing by his father's side. When the Delaware boy saw Peter, he ran up to him.

"My father told me you were leaving with him," Little Wolf said, "and I begged to come along. Here is your horse."

He gave Peter a boost up on a small chestnut mare and mounted a horse of his own. Captain Peter put Christian Post's letter to the general in his saddlebag and they were on their way.

"God go with you," Christian Post called out as they started across the glade. A lump formed in Peter's throat as he turned once more to glimpse the tall missionary standing along the edge of the village, waving.

They rode across the glade and past the wood-carver's lodge. Everything had happened so quickly that Peter had had not time to say good-bye to Bluebird and her grandfather. He looked for them now as they passed the lodge, but they were nowhere in sight. He thought of the carving of Joseph he had left behind and hoped that Christian Post would give it to Bluebird.

They rode through the woods, following the portage path which paralleled the river. A mist crept up from the marshland and hung in thick bands across their trail. Peter could see only the legs of the horses in front of him.

They rode for many miles then stopped at an opening in the forest. While they squatted on the riverbank to wait for the horses to water, Little Wolf said, "My brother must be happy that he is returning to his home over the mountains."

Peter nodded a silent reply.

"My father and I shall miss you," Little Wolf continued. "Our White Brother, who stays behind, will miss you, too. Bluebird and her grandfather will be asking about you."

Peter stared blankly at the wisps of fog swirling over the dark water. He had not realized how much of a family they had become to him and how much he, too, would miss them.

Later in the day the fog lifted and through the bare trees, they could see the Shawnee village of Sacunk. As they passed the grim, bark houses, Peter wondered if the prisoner who was to be burned had been saved and if he, too, would be set free. A short distance downstream a long stretch of moving water came into view and Peter knew that they had come to the Ohio.

But they did not follow the big river southward as he had expected. Captain Peter chose a trail leading eastward away from the river. When daylight faded in the forest and it started to rain, they were happy to find a wide ledge of rocks under which to make camp.

With flint and steel Captain Peter soon had a warm fire going. Peter leaned back against the rocky wall of their cave and listened to the hollow sound of the wind through the forest. Somewhere on the rocks above them a wolf howled. Peter pulled his robe closer around him as he listened to the lonesome wail.

But it was warm and cozy under the rock ledge with the fire popping and he snuggled up to it and soon fell sound asleep.

It seemed like only a short time later that Captain Peter was shaking him awake. The boys shivered in the cold gray dawn as they folded their robes and flung them on the backs of the hobbled horses. The rain had stopped but the sky was heavy with gray clouds as they started out. Along the horizon to the east where the sky touched the earth the rising sun through the clouds showed a deep red as if the edge of the forest was afire.

They followed a narrow trail over rolling, heavily timbered hills, broken now and then with clearings of rye grass and cedar. When they came to a wide, rapid stream, Peter decided that this must be the upper waters of the Allegheny.

Captain Peter found a stony place to ford the river and they rode on through the endless forest until their trail joined a wide rutted road leading westward. The chief got off his horse to examine the muddy tracks on the road.

"Old Traders' Path," he said. "The general and his men have traveled along this way not many suns ago."

Peter's heart leaped. "Will this road lead us to the general's camp at Turtle Creek?"

Captain Peter nodded and mounted his big roan. They turned their horses westward and studied the hoofprints as they rode along. The land was rolling, filled with ravines and well timbered slopes, and Peter had a strange feeling that he had been on this same road before. Could this be the trail his Indian captors had used when they brought him and Sally Turner to Fort Duquesne, he wondered.

Up ahead Captain Peter stopped suddenly and sat rigid on his horse, sniffing the air.

The boys reined in their mounts and sniffed too. There was a faint, acrid scent of burning wood somewhere in the forest.

Captain Peter kicked his horse to a trot and the boys urged their own mounts on. It wasn't long before they glimpsed through the trees the thin, gray lines of smoke from campfires ahead.

13
The Camp at
Turtle Creek

Along the banks of Turtle Creek, hidden in a long, deep gorge, they found the general's camp. They stopped their horses on top of the gorge and looked down.

The entire ravine was filled with bright little campfires. A Provincial sentry in a buff and blue uniform moved to and fro underneath the leafless sycamores. As Peter stared at the once familiar sight of soldiers and wagons, a feeling of joy and excitement welled up inside him.

Heedless of Captain Peter's warning, he nudged the chestnut mare down the steep bank. She skidded over loose shale and stones and halfway down the bank her hoofs caught in a brier. With a loud whinny she plunged to a sudden stop. Snorting and thrashing about wildly to get loose from the brier, she pitched Peter from the saddle and he fell headlong into a laurel thicket.

He sat up, rubbing his head and at the same time staring at the pair of muddy boots that were planted in front of him. He struggled to his feet and gaped at the long rifle pointed directly at him. His thoughts were confused as he looked at the unfriendly soldier holding the rifle. Couldn't the man see that he was a white boy who had been a captive of the Delawares?

The sentry took a step forward and thrust the barrel of the rifle into Peter's stomach.

"Wait—wait!" the boy gasped.

At that moment a hand from behind came down quickly on the rifle barrel, jerking it away from Peter.

"We come as friends," Captain Peter's voice spoke out behind him.

"Friends!" shouted the sentry. "You are bloody Indians. That's what you are!"

A big, stormy-looking man dressed in tartan and kilts came hurrying up to see what the commotion was. "Indians did you say, Johnson?" the Highlander roared with alarm. His eyes under a pair of black, shaggy eyebrows went suddenly narrow. "Sneaking into camp, are you! Aye, the general will hear about this!"

"But—but—" Peter sputtered. Dismayed, he dropped his eyes to his fringed hunting jacket and moccasins with the wolf design embroidered on them. It was no use to try to convince them who he

*Snorting and thrashing about wildly, the mare pitched
Peter headlong into a laurel thicket.*

was. He had forgotten how much like an Indian he must look by now. His face was as brown with the sun and wind as Little Wolf's and his auburn hair, now darkened with bear's grease and soot, hung down his neck as black and straight as any Indian boy's.

Captain Peter took a step forward. He held out the palms of his hands in a greeting of friendship. "We come as friends. We bring a message to the English chief from our White Brother."

The Scotsman sized up the tall, dignified chief standing before him. "A message from the White Brother?" he asked. "Could this White Brother be a man called Christian Post?"

Captain Peter nodded and drew the letter from his saddlebag.

The Highlander took the letter. "I am Mac-Cochran, aide to the general," he said. "Leave your horses here with the sentry and come along with me."

Leaving the sentry staring wide-eyed after them, they followed MacCochran down the bank and into the camp. It was late afternoon and the long shadows of night had already settled in the gorge. Along the banks of Turtle Creek cook fires blinked through the dusk. Shadowy forms of soldiers moved to and fro between crude lean-tos made of saplings and pine boughs.

The Highlander led them to a tent in the middle of the camp. He pulled back the tent flap and in the smoky light of a rush candle Peter glimpsed a frail-looking officer in a red military coat lying on a cot.

The officer sat up when they entered the tent, his pale face close to the candlelight. By the set of his jaw and the determined look in his eyes, Peter knew at once that this must be old "Iron Head" himself.

General Forbes studied each one of them curiously. "Well, MacCochran, who are these Indians and what do they want?"

The Highlander stepped forward and handed the sealed letter to the general. "They have brought a message from Christian Post, sir," he said.

The general hastily broke the seal and held the letter close to the flame. As he read, a look of satisfaction spread across his sallow face.

"MacCochran, these Delawares bring good news from their White Brother—news we have been waiting for. The Ohio Indians have accepted Teedyuscung's peace treaty. They have laid down their tomahawks against us and will not fight with the French to hold the Forks of the Ohio. Christian Post with his peace talks has performed a miracle!"

The aide's eyes shone in the flame light. "Aye, sir!" he agreed happily. "Now victory will be ours."

General Forbes turned back to the letter and Peter watched him anxiously. He knew by the general's expression that he was reading the part Christian Post had written about him.

Forbes looked up from the letter at the two boys standing by his cot. "Which one of you is Peter Andreas?"

Peter stepped forward. The general studied him closely.

"You have blue eyes, lad," he observed. "I should have noticed that sooner. Christian Post asks us to escort you to your home in Path Valley. Perhaps it would be best if you stay with Captain Peter and your young friend here until our campaign is over. Then

127

we will see that you get safely over the mountains."

"Thank you, sir," Peter said. Then he ventured boldly, "There's another captive at Fort Duquesne, sir. Her name is Sally Turner and—"

"I know, Peter," the general broke in wearily, "You would like to find her. Well, lad, if that is at all possible, she shall accompany you back to the settlements. According to the treaty the French and Indians will be bringing all their captives to Fort Duquesne to be released to the army. It may take many days for them to arrive but do not fear. You shall all be returned to your homes in due time."

Forbes returned to Christian Post's letter and a heavy silence fell over the little group as they waited for him to speak again. Outside the gloomy forest had deepened into night and the little campfires gleamed brighter than ever. From one of the fires came the notes of a nostalgic ballad sung to the mournful whine of a bagpipe. The thin strains drifted through the camp as homesick soldiers bedded down on the cold ground for the night.

Then somewhere across the distant hills a dull, ominous, booming sound echoed through the dim forest. The song stopped abruptly and the bagpipe whined to one last wail. The camp fell silent as the strange explosion reverberated again and again over the western hills.

General Forbes looked up quickly from the letter.

"MacCochran," he ordered, "see if you can find out what that explosion was. It sounded like cannon!"

The big Highlander fairly flew from the tent. In a short time he came hurrying back, his face grim and puzzled.

"Well, what was it?" General Forbes demanded. "From what direction did it come?"

"It seemed to have come from the west," Mac-Cochran reported breathlessly.

"Would you say it might have come from Fort Duquesne?"

"Aye, sir." MacCochran nodded. "The sentries seem to think so, sir."

"From such a distance it must have been quite an explosion," the general mused.

"Aye, sir, that's what one sentry reported," Mac-Cochran answered. "The man said it sounded as if the French at the fort might have fired all their cannon at once."

The general turned to Captain Peter. "Why would the French be firing their cannon at this time of night?"

The lines on the chief's dark face deepened in thought. "It could mean that the white father is welcoming reinforcements from Canada," he replied. "They fire their cannon at such a time."

Peter and Little Wolf exchanged anxious glances.

Forbes struggled to rise from his cot. "If that sound came from Fort Duquesne, the French are up to something and I don't like it one bit," he said in a troubled voice.

MacCochran hurried to his side to help him up. "What shall we do, sir?" he asked.

"What shall we do!" echoed the general, pacing back and forth in the tent. "We shall look the dragon right in the mouth, MacCochran. Christian Post has sent us the news we have been waiting for. Now we must act! We shall march for the Forks of the Ohio first thing in the morning."

He turned to Captain Peter. "You know the French fort better than any one of us, chief. Would you help us when we get there? The lads will be safe riding with my litter."

Captain Peter replied, "I will help you, but I will not fight with your men. Our White Brother has taught us to live in peace, even with our enemies."

Respect for the chief's words shone on the general's face. "I do not ask you to fight, Captain Peter, only to help us peacefully." Then his blue eyes blazing with determination, he said to the little group around him, "Before another night passes, gentlemen, we shall be sleeping in Fort Duquesne!"

Peter's heart leaped at the general's words. He knew now why John Forbes' men called him "Head of Iron."

The general went on with his instructions. "Mac-Cochran, tell Bouquet, Montgomery, and Washington to come here at once, and see that Captain Peter and these boys have food and shelter for the night."

MacCochran saluted smartly and led the way out of the general's tent to a place in the camp where there was an empty lean-to. He brought them tin plates of salt pork and cornmeal bread. Little Wolf had borrowed a hot coal from a nearby fire and started a pile of sticks smoking in front of the crude shelter.

The night was bitter cold with the feel of storm in the air. After they had scraped their tin plates clean, Captain Peter built up the fire and hunched over it in silence. Peter knew what the chief was thinking. It was the same thing the general and everybody in camp must be wondering about.

What were those strange booming sounds that had echoed through the dark forest that night? Had the French fired all their cannon to welcome reinforcements from Canada? What would the next day bring on the march to the Forks of the Ohio?

14
The March to
Fort Duquesne

Peter awoke to the sounds of men breaking camp. Notes of reveille from a bugle echoed against the long tumbling walls of the gorge. Shouts of command pierced the cold morning air. Horses stamped and whinnied shrilly. A wave of excitement crept over Peter. Today he would be marching to Fort Duquesne with General Forbes' army!

He shivered in his buckskins and huddled closer to the fire. Tongues of flames lapped at the cold gray mist that hung over the lean-to. More than ever there was the feeling of storm in the air.

MacCochran came striding up to their shelter with

breakfast. Across his shoulder was slung a long Pennsylvania rifle. He reached for the rifle and held it out to Captain Peter. "The general gives you this rifle as a gift, chief."

Captain Peter drew back when he saw the weapon, but MacCochran went on to explain, "He doesn't ask you to fire it at the enemy. He gives it in appreciation for your marching with the army to Fort Duquesne."

Captain Peter took the rifle and fingered it fondly. Little Wolf's eyes shone as he watched his father. The curly maple stock shone with a deep, rich glow. The long barrel was as smooth as cold satin. Both white men and Indians knew that the Pennsylvania rifle was a prized possession and the most beautiful firearm in America.

"Tell the general that I thank him for this fine gift. It will make the hunting of bear and deer much easier," the chief said. MacCochran nodded and hurried on about his errands.

Captain Peter put the rifle aside and prepared to break camp. "Find our horses," he told the boys.

The camp was in a state of confusion and Peter and Little Wolf did not know where to look for the horses first.

"The white men buzz about like a swarm of bees," Peter remarked.

Little Wolf laughed. "You talk like an Indian, my brother. I was thinking the same thing."

They found the horses hobbled with the teams used to pull the swivel guns. By the time they got them back to the lean-to, the soldiers were already forming their lines of march. At commands from the officers, the drums beat a rousing cadence and the

pipes struck up *Blaz Sron* as the brigade began its
march out of the gorge and along the old Traders'
Path to the Forks of the Ohio.

"The white man makes much noise when he
marches to his enemy," Little Wolf said. "When the
Indian goes through the forest to find his enemy, he
walks as silent and as crafty as the lynx."

The boys and the chief rode with MacCochran and
the general, who was carried on a litter slung between
two horses. The general's face was pale and drawn
with pain from the stomach disorder he had suffered
all the way across the mountains. Yet he would not remain in camp. He was determined to be with his
army when they marched to Fort Duquesne.

The troops followed in three long parallel columns.
MacCochran explained the order to Captain Peter
and the boys.

"The middle column is Colonel Montgomery's
Highlanders," the Scotsman said proudly, pointing
back to the column of marching men, their red tunics
and plaid kilts adding a splash of bright color to the
gray forest. "Colonel Henry Bouquet's Royal
Americans are on the left. They're the lads wearing
scarlet coats faced with blue. The Provincials are on
the right in the green uniforms. They're the First
Pennsylvania Battalion commanded by Colonel John
Armstrong. Behind the Pennsylvanians are the
Virginians, commanded by Colonel George
Washington."

Peter's eyes lingered on the young officer dressed
in buckskins, his body tall in the saddle. He
remembered Daniel Boone and the men of the
wagon brigade talking about this young Virginia

134

colonel. The Buckskin Colonel, they called him, and the rugged Provincials fighting under him were called Long Knives became of the long hunting knives they carried on their belts. They were the best Indian fighters in America, Daniel Boone had said, far better than the more disciplined English troops. They had proved that fact when they had marched over the mountains with General Braddock three years ago.

As the army pushed through the dense forest, someone started up an old marching song and soon every soldier joined in the chorus. Only John Forbes remained silent and thoughtful as he jostled along on his litter. Anxiously he glanced at the clouds brooding overhead. The air remained cold and damp; the storm was coming. He announced that he could feel it in his aching body.

The lusty voices of Forbes' men continued as the army marched over the low foothills that dipped downward to the Ohio Valley. Toward the middle of the day the storm broke. Frozen drops of sleet beat against bare tree trunks and rattled on dead oak leaves. The cold pellets stung the faces of the marching men. The soldiers slipped their powder bags inside their shirts to keep them dry and hunched their shoulders against the cold wind.

From time to time MacCochran glanced anxiously at the general who looked more ill than ever. The long cold march had increased the pains in his stomach and his face was distorted with suffering. The faithful aide bent over the litter to ask, "Wouldn't it be wise, sir, to stop for a rest?"

"Nonsense, MacCochran," replied old Iron Head.

"We must keep moving. At this snail's pace, we'll do well to reach the Forks of the Ohio before nightfall."

The march continued on through the storm. By late afternoon they finally reached the rise of land overlooking the Forks. The general called a halt, and as Peter looked down at the gloomy plain below, he was reminded of that summer day when the old chief had stopped the captives and had pointed to the triangle of land where the rivers meet.

"*De-un-da-ga*," he had called it and that name still rang horror in Peter's mind.

He fidgeted in his saddle. The chestnut mare pawed the ground and snorted impatiently as they waited for further orders. Peter strained his eyes to the Point. The freezing rain had stopped but the five arrowhead-shaped bastions of Fort Duquesne were hidden in a cold white mist that covered the entire river valley. In its white shroud, the French fort waited for its enemy, silent and foreboding.

The general surveyed the scene from his litter. "Captain Peter," he asked, "where are the exact locations of the outer defenses and the Indian camp?"

Captain Peter explained the lay of the land to Forbes and his officers. Then the general commanded Captain John Haslet and his dragoons to ride ahead in advance of the marching men to reconnoiter the Forks. Peter felt a surge of excitement as he watched the horsemen plunge down the hill and disappear across the misty flats.

"When we proceed, we shall do so with caution," Forbes warned his other officers. "Captain de Ligneris might see fit to welcome us with his cannon."

The officers smiled thinly at the general's remark

and returned to their regiments. With the muffled tap of a single drum the army proceeded slowly down the hill to the river flats.

His nerves tingling, Peter urged the chestnut mare to follow. Ahead the foot soldiers were stumbling over hidden rocks as they pushed their way through the plum thicket that covered the steep hillside.

When they finally reached the flats, the general ordered Colonel Armstrong to sound three volleys from his gun. The shots echoed over the wintry river bluffs as the army waited for a return volley of gunfire from the fort. But only an ominous silence greeted them from below.

"It is strange the French father does not return the gunfire," Little Wolf said with a puzzled frown.

Slowly the army continued its march across the desolate, marshy land. Ahead dried cornstalks reared up like ghostly forms in the mist. Every tree, every bush, every rock took on a menacing form in the late afternoon gloom. At any moment Peter expected to hear the war cries of the braves from the Indian camp. The skin of his neck prickled at the thought of meeting those fearful warriors face to face, and he urged his mount closer to Captain Peter's horse.

They rode past the gardens and now they could make out the misty outlines of the thirty wigwams of the Indian camp. As they came closer, Peter was surprised to see no smoke rising from the smoke holes. Was the Indian camp deserted or was this a trick, he wondered.

Suddenly the advance came to a halt and out of the half-light the form of a man on horseback galloped toward the general's litter. MacCochran reached for his claymore but Captain Peter held up his hand. "It's a redcoat," he said.

The dragoon wheeled his horse to a stop and saluted briskly. "Sir, Captain Haslet reports that the fort is quiet. We have approached as far as the outer defenses and have seen nor heard nothing."

The general was thoughtful. "What does Captain Haslet think?" he asked.

"The captain thinks it is a bit spooky, sir," the dragoon replied.

Forbes nodded. "They may be waiting to ambush us from the rear. I have heard that Captain de Ligneris is full of tricks."

Turning to Captain Peter, he asked, "What do you think, chief?"

Captain Peter nodded agreement to what the general had said.

"Very well," Forbes concluded. "we shall march upon the fort as planned. MacCochran, ride ahead and tell Colonel Washington and Colonel Armstrong to advance their regiments cautiously. Colonel Montgomery and Colonel Bouquet will be the rear guard. We shall soon find out whether or not Captain de Ligneris is up to any of his tricks."

"Old Iron Head paused and looked solemnly at his aide. "Tell the colonels that there will be no retreat this time from Fort Duquesne!"

After MacCochran had carried out the general's orders, the advance started ahead again. The Provincials, their rifles ready, followed, melting into dim shadows as they skirted the Indian camp. With the tap of a drum the Highlanders marched in open formation, the danger of cannon fire from the fort becoming greater with each step they took.

By now the advance must be within sight of the outer defenses, Peter thought. Why hadn't the French fired on them? How far would Captain de Ligneris let the English go?

Peter's nerves tingled. The suspense was maddening. He wished there was something he could do. What would Christian Post do if he were here? he wondered.

"He would pray," Peter decided. "I could do that!" He reined in his horse and bowed his head. "Please God, let no lives be lost today. Let this battle be settled . . ."

Wild cries from the direction of Colonel Montgomery's regiment broke through Peter's prayer. He lifted his head and looked around him. The general was sitting up on his litter, his eyes staring. "I hope the Highlanders haven't fallen into some kind of trap!" he exclaimed. "Things have been too quiet at the fort to suit me. Ride ahead again, Mac-Cochran, and see what's the matter."

John Forbes paused and frowned at his aide. "Mac-Cochran, did you hear me?"

But at that moment MacCochran seemed dumb to everything around him as he leaned over in his saddle to examine something along the well-worn path that led to the palisades. When he finally did look up, his mouth was a tight line and his eyes were blazing.

"I can tell you what's the matter, sir," he muttered.

Peter and Little Wolf's eyes darted ahead to where the Highlander was pointing. There, bordering the path, were stakes on which were placed the heads of the Highland prisoners belonging to General Braddock's army, their blood-stained kilts draped below, a grim reminder to the English of what had happened to the attackers of Fort Duquesne before them!

Peter's stomach turned over as he stared in horror at the gruesome sight. So this was how it was in battle!

Now he understood why Brother Joseph and the Moravians hated war and why missionaries like Christian Post and his parents risked their lives in the camps of the Delawares to teach brotherhood and peace.

It was war that had set the French against the English and the Indians against his own people. It was war which had deprived him of his parents and Indians of their families. He had suffered no more than they. His loss was no greater than theirs. The feeling of hate and fear left Peter's heart. Was it not better to risk one's life in peace than in war? he thought as he turned away from the grisly sight.

MacCochran's face was crimson with rage. "If there's any bloody bluecoats in the fort now, sir, there won't be anything left of them after the Highlanders get done with them!"

Forbes ordered his aides to push ahead to the outer defenses. When they arrived, they could see the Highlanders boosting one another over the palisades of the hornwork. Peter held his breath. Surely now the guns in the bastions would explode!

Colonel Washington was desperately trying to get his regiment to take cover. His bay horse reared as he shouted commands to his men. Squatting behind trees and bushes, the Provincials held their rifles posed in readiness to back up the Highlanders. But still not a cannon nor rifle shot sounded from the fort.

Peter's heart beat fast as he glimpsed the first of the daring Highlanders drop over the top of the blackened logs in the palisade. The silence that followed was almost too much for the men crouched in waiting to bear. Then a hoarse cry from inside the fort brought every waiting soldier to his feet.

The next moment the gate in the hornwork was thrown open revealing the charred remains of the outlying barracks and the dark mass of the fort itself at the very tip of the Point.

"The French are gone!" rang out the hoarse cries from inside the palisade. "The fort's been burned!"

15
God's Plan for Peter

At the cry of the Highlanders, the Royal Americans and Provincials broke ranks and rushed through the palisades and into the ruins of Fort Duquesne. Captain Peter wheeled his horse around and galloped after them, the boys following not far behind.

The damp air was heavy with the acrid smell of smoldering logs. Only the stone chimneys of the larger cabins along the Monongahela and the log walls to the land front were left standing. The star-shaped stockade carved out of the green of the wilderness valley was now only a black design of charred timbers and smoke.

"Everything is gone!" gasped Little Wolf. "The French father has left nothing but an ugly scar on the earth."

His words were dimmed by the pipers who struck up *Blaz Sron* again as General Forbes entered the smoldering ruins. Captain Haslet rode up to meet him.

"Are you certain that the enemy is gone?" the general asked.

"Yes, sir," Captain Haslet assured him. "My men have searched everywhere. There is not a Frenchman left."

The general managed to lift himself up on one elbow. A smile of satisfaction crept over his pale face. "A very pleasant situation," he told his officers. "Gentlemen, we have achieved the greatest victory any army can achieve because on this day, November 25, 1758, we have occupied the Forks of the Ohio without having to fire a single shot at the enemy!"

A cry of "Huzza!" filled the air. With Mac-Cochran's help, Forbes raised himself to a sitting position and looked over the ruins of the once formidable fort.

"See if one of you can run up a flag of some kind," he told his officers. "We'll want to rebuild the fort. I'd like the new fort to be named in the honor of our good Prime Minister, William Pitt, and I do so name it Fort Pitt and this junction of rivers, Pittsburgh."

Again a cry of "Huzza!" went up as the name Pittsburgh echoed through the great river valley. The new name for the Forks of the Ohio had a good solid ring to it, Peter thought, a name he hoped would last

143

forever in the Ohio Valley.

Sir John St. Clair, the quartermaster general, brought a folded flag from his saddlebag and presented it to the general. Turning to his colonels, Forbes chose George Washington to raise the flag.

Peter's eyes followed the young Buckskin Colonel as he walked up to the general and bent his broad shoulders over the litter to receive the flag. With wide strides he mounted the smoke-blackened mound of dirt where the flag bastion had been and ran up the Union Jack on a pole.

As the English flag rose over the fallen timbers of Fort Duquesne, George Washington took off his tricornered hat, letting the biting wind blow through his sandy locks. With quiet happiness he watched the red and white crosses of St. George and St. Andrew blow out against the gray autumn sky where once the Lilies of France had waved so boldly.

During the brief ceremony at the flag bastion, two ragged, half-starved men wandered through the British lines. Their eyes had a dazed look as they staggered up to the general's litter. MacCochran stepped quickly in front of them. "Your names!" he commanded.

One of the men stumbled forward. "Jonas Smith, sir, of General Braddock's colonial militia," he said in a hoarse voice, not much more than a whisper. His companion saluted smartly. "Benjamin Graham, sir, of Major Grant's Highland Brigade."

"Where have you come from?" General Forbes asked.

"From the riverbank where we have been hiding," Benjamin Graham replied. "We were prisoners who escaped from the French. Oh, sir, it's good to see our countrymen again!"

"It's good to have you with us again," Forbes told the prisoners. "Did Captain de Ligneris destroy the fort?"

"Aye, sir," Jonas Smith spoke up. "When he got word that the Ohio Indians had made peace with the English, he knew the jig was up."

"Then when his scouts informed him that your forces, sir, were camped at Turtle Creek, only a day's march from the Forks of the Ohio, Captain de Ligneris decided to give up the fort and leave at once," Benjamin Graham continued. "But before he left, he burned the fort so as not to leave it for the enemy."

"Aye," murmured Jonas Smith. "It was a way out for them when they knew they was cornered."

General Forbes looked around at the bare, smoky ruins. "Have the French left us anything?"

The men shook their heads. "Not a thing, sir," Jonas Smith answered. "They had the cannon and powder put in bateaux which were sent down the Ohio to the Illinois territory. With them went the prisoners—all except the ones they gave to their Indians to torture and kill and us two who managed to escape. The other bateaux carried the French soldiers and their families up the Allegheny to Fort Machault and several soldiers left by land for Presque Isle on Lake Erie."

"Then when everyone was gone," Benjamin continued, "the captain set fire to the fort last night. The roofs were removed from the houses so that they would burn fast. When the fire reached the powder

145

magazine where fifty or sixty barrels of spoiled powder had been left, the whole fort blew up."

"The land around trembled with the explosion," Jonas added, shaking his head at the thought. "We thought we were being blown to kingdom come!"

"That must have been the explosion we heard last night at Turtle Creek," General Forbes said. "We were wondering what mischief the French were up to. How did you two manage to escape?"

"Well, sir," Benjamin said, "when we found out that the French were going to hand over most of the men prisoners to their Indians, we volunteered to help the soldiers move the heavy cannon onto the bateaux. That way we escaped being tortured and killed."

"In the confusion of the work," Jonas continued, "we skedaddled off and hid under the riverbank. We tried to help the other prisoners escape but it was too late; so we just burrowed us a cave out of the bank and hid there until we heard your bagpipes. It was a mighty welcome sound to hear, sir."

Forbes turned to his quartermaster general. "St. Clair, see that these men get warm clothing and food."

The prisoners turned to leave but before they went off with the quartermaster general, Jonas Smith fell on his knees by Forbes' litter and with tears of gratitude running down his sooty cheeks, he exclaimed, "Thank you, sir. Oh, thank you!"

His companion helped him to his feet and both men hobbled off with Sir John St. Clair.

A sudden snow squall deepened the dusk of the river valley and Forbes ordered his men to build shelters out of the half-burned timbers. "There'll be plenty of work to do tonight to make these ruins into a suitable camp," he told his soldiers.

And later, as Peter was dropping off to sleep in a crude lean-to he had helped Captain Peter and Little Wolf make, he thought wearily, "There'll be plenty of work to do here tomorrow, too, and the next day and many days after that!"

Daylight had barely broken through the English camp the next morning when the ring of axes felling trees for the new Fort Pitt echoed through the river valley. Peter awoke early with the others and started out for Captain Haslet's shelter where the two French prisoners had been quartered. He had something important to ask Jonas Smith and Benjamin Graham.

When he found the two men, he hardly recognized them. They were dressed in warm uniforms from extra clothing the quartermaster general had given them. They had been well fed and their drawn, frightened faces were relaxed as they sat by a fire, talking with their countrymen.

Peter stood by until there was a break in the conversation. Then he stepped forward.

"Sirs," he asked, "did you know a girl named Sally Turner in Fort Duquesne? She was taken captive by the Indians the same time I was, but they sold her to a French captain and his wife."

The two men looked at one another thoughtfully.

"Do you know who the lass might be, Jonas?"

"I'm thinking, Ben." Then Jonas's eyes brightened. "Was she a pretty little gal with long, honey-colored hair?"

Peter nodded eagerly. "That would be Sally!"

"Ah, yes," Jonas recalled. "Captain Homet and his missus sure did make a fuss over that gal, for a fact. Dressed her all up in them fancy dresses and put ribbons in her hair. Treated her like she was their own daughter. They wouldn't let her get near the other prisoners."

"What—what happened to her?" Peter asked impatiently.

"Why, she left the fort with them and the other families who was heading up the Allegheny to Fort Machault." Jonas winked his eye at Peter and smiled. "I wouldn't fret none about her, lad. She was a spunky little gal, for a fact, and I heard tell she had no family anymore in the settlements. I'll wager if she had the choice to go back to the settlements or to stay with her new family, she would choose to stay with the Homets. I reckon the only sorrow she had was for the rest of us who didn't fare near as good as her."

Peter thanked Jonas and walked on through the ruins of the fort. At the Point he climbed down the steep drop of sandy bank and walked out on the sandspit. It was here Little Wolf had brought him the day he had come to the fort to help Sally escape. He would never know why he couldn't find her that day, but he was relieved to know that she was safe and happy in her new home.

The cold wind rippled the gray waters of the Ohio. Across the Monongahela the trees stood gray and bleak against the steep bluffs that rose up behind them. He turned and looked across the Allegheny to the island where he had first met Christian Post.

Peter marveled at what the Moravian missionary

had accomplished. Alone he had done what General Braddock and the entire English army had not been able to do. With no other weapon than a Bible, Christian Post had won over the French Indians and had brought peace to the Ohio Valley.

Now the settlers in the back country could live without fear, and in the wilderness of the Ohio country Christian Post could build his mission, in peace too. "It was truly God's will," Peter told himself.

Then he wondered, "What is God's plan for me?" He turned with a sigh and started up the sandy bank toward the English camp, not knowing yet what he would do with his life nor what God really wanted of him.

His thoughts were interrupted by the cry of the sentry on duty. Peter looked to where the soldier was pointing. Several canoes filled with Indians were coming across the river.

The warning of the sentry spread rapidly through the camp. Soldiers dropped their axes and grabbed up their muskets.

"They're taking no chances," Peter told himself as he hurried to the riverbank to see who the Indians were and what they wanted.

Captain Peter and Little Wolf were by Colonel Bouquet's side when the Indians beached their canoes on the sandy bank. All were relieved when their leader held out the palms of his hands in friendly greeting. He was a Delaware and as Peter edged his way through the gathering, he could make out some of the words the Indian spoke.

He was telling Captain Peter that he and his tribe wished to live in peace with their brothers, the redcoats. Before they returned north to their winter lodges, they would hunt and fish and provide food for the English camp.

"Tell him that we, too, wish to live in peace with his tribe," Colonel Bouquet told Captain Peter. "Tell their chief that we thank him."

The colonel ordered gifts to be brought from the quartermaster's tent. He gave the Delawares gunpowder and clothes and wampum. Pleased with the gifts, the Indians left the English camp and returned to their own camp across the river.

As Peter and Little Wolf watched them go, Little Wolf said, "My father and I will be leaving for Kuskuski when the sun again rises. If you still wish to stay here with your own people, I have no right to say a word, but I will be sad to say good-bye to my brother."

Peter saw real sorrow in Little Wolf's face which moved him deeply. He turned away. It would be sad for him, too, to have to say good-bye to his Indian brother. He had no words now to express how he felt. Perhaps tomorrow he could find the words to say good-bye to his friends.

But when morning came and Peter joined Mac-Cochran in the corral to see Little Wolf and Captain Peter off, words of farewell still eluded him. Little Wolf put his hands on Peter's shoulders in one last gesture of friendship. His face was sad and he turned quickly and mounted his horse.

Peter's voice broke with emotion when he tried to say farewell. He could only raise his hand to wave as he watched his Indian friends walk their horses slowly out of camp.

At that moment Peter knew what he must do. "I'll be a wood-carver and a missionary like my father," he thought.

As he watched them make their way around the stumps of the recently felled trees, Peter thought of the village they were returning to. He thought of Christian Post and Muchomes. The vision of Bluebird's face, overflowing with kindness and understanding, rose up before his eyes. He thought of how happy she would have been if he had stayed to finish the Christmas putz for her. And then he knew why he could not say good-bye to Little Wolf.

He plunged his hands into his buckskin jacket and brought out the Christmas lamb his father had carved for him. He stared down at it, excitement stirring inside him as he remembered Brother Joseph's words: "The lamb is a symbol of peace and brotherhood, the two virtues the Moravians love most."

Was this why his father had carved the lamb for him? The realization burned within Peter like a revelation. Peace and brotherhood—a lamb in the wilderness! And at that moment Peter knew what he must do, what his mission in life would be.

"I will be a wood-carver—a wood-carver and a missionary like my father," he thought. He knew now for certain that this was God's plan for him, to spread peace and brotherhood to his Indian brothers just as his father and mother had done.

Peter felt a thrill of joy he had never felt before. He turned and faced the big Highlander standing by his side. "MacCochran, will you give the general a message to give to my uncle, Matthew Boyd, of Path Valley?" he asked.

Breathlessly he told the aide that he had decided to return to Kuskuski with Christian Post. "I want my uncle to know that I am alive and well," he said.

152

"Whoa, lad," protested the astonished Scotsman. "Are you sure that's what you want?"

"I'm sure," Peter replied, and the radiant look on the boy's face dismissed any further doubts Mac-Cochran might have had.

"I'll tell the general, lad. Now find your horse."

Peter wasted no time in finding the little chestnut mare. MacCochran helped him to mount. "Now be off with you before I get my senses back!" the big Highlander ordered.

Peter urged the little mare on a trot across the river flats. When Captain Peter and Little Wolf looked back and saw him coming, they reined in their mounts to wait for him. Little Wolf gave a whoop of joy and trotted back across the flats to meet him. *"Kschamehhellan!"* he called out happily.

The three rode together up the hill overlooking the Forks of the Ohio. At the top they glanced back at the blackened ruins of Fort Duquesne, its logs still smoldering—the end of one white man's reign and the beginning of another's.

The trail dipped downward and soon the ugly, blackened pattern in the wilderness was out of sight. No longer was the stench of charred wood in the air— only the cold, pine-scented fragrance of the forest.

Peter turned his eyes to the west. His heart sang. He was going home to where the sun was his father and the earth was his mother.

RUTH NULTON MOORE was born in Easton, Pennsylvania, and now lives in Bethlehem, Pennsylvania, with her husband, a professor of accounting at Lehigh University, and their two sons, Carl and Stephen.

Specializing in English literature, she received a BA degree from Bucknell University and an MA from Columbia University. She did post graduate work at the University of Pittsburgh.

Mrs. Moore taught English and social studies in Wilson Borough High School in Easton and in the secondary schools in Detroit, Michigan. She has been writing since she was ten years old and her first poems were published when she was fifteen;

She has written poetry and stories for *Children's Activities* and *Jack and Jill*. One of her stories has been adapted in an elementary school reader (*High and Wide*, Book 3-1, American Book Company, 1968) and several reading workbooks. She is author of the following books: *Frisky, the Playful Pony* (Criterion) which has been translated into Swedish (Walstroms Bokforlag), *Hiding the Bell* (Westminster Press), *Peace Treaty*, (Herald Press), and *The Ghost Bird Mystery* (Herald Press).

She teaches third-grade Sunday school at Christ Church, United Church of Christ, Bethlehem, and helps her family with a small farm, High Meadows, in the Endless Mountains of Pennsylvania.